STOLEN LIVES

by

Hiam Mondini

written on a Blackberry Classic

for Miriam

INTRODUCTION

I can't believe it! The blue cross I've been dreaming about so long is there on the stick! I never could have imagined how happy this makes me feel! I could scream, cry, cheer and squeal all at the same time! My heart is beating like crazy and I feel sick as a dog.

What now? What should I do? I have to tell my husband, but how? I could buy baby clothes and give them to him as a present. Or I could leave him a message with a photo of the test. What is my boss going to say, will I be able to keep my job? A nanny? Day care... oh god, strangers around my children? I hope everything is alright with the baby. Did I start taking folic acid soon enough? What if it has Down Syndrome, will he want to keep it? I would never have an abortion, but would I be able to raise a child alone? We've waited so long, I can't have anything go wrong.

Somebody knocks at the door and yells, "Hey, how long are you going to be in there? Other people have to go, too!" I have forgotten where I am in all the excitement. I gather everything up, apologize to the women who are waiting, and hurry out of the cafe in the big Swiss city, but where to first?

CHAPTER 1

Waves smash powerfully against the posts of the pier. It stinks of musty sand, dead fish and seagull shit. The sea is angry and loud, the clouds hurry across the sky, and the joggers on the Coney Island beach have pulled their hoods tight around their faces to protect them from the cold.

Frank is among the people on the beach today. He hasn't done any exercise in a long while and the holidays have left their mark on his waistline. Freja, his Bordeaux mastiff with a Danish first name, has been unhappy with him ever since he reduced his long beach runs to a minimum. He has made a New Year's resolution for the sake of both of them. Since turning 50 he hasn't managed to stick to it, but this year is going to be different!

"Freja! Come here, old girl! Where have you gotten to? Freja, no games in this weather! Freja!" He hears whimpering and whining, the barking of an excited dog then Freja runs round his legs, jumps up at him, almost knocks him over, moves away again and disappears. "Freja, what has gotten into you? Get back here, now!"

Frank can hardly see anything in the dark below the pier. Then the acrid stink hits him and he almost throws up. What the hell is under there? It is making Freja nervous and upset, which isn't a good sign, because thankfully his pet doesn't like dead animals...

"911. What's your emergency?"

CHAPTER 2

It must be intuition. Just as I pick up my cell phone to call Rob, it hums and I open the message, "Let's meet at 7 at the Italian restaurant! If I'm late, just get me a calzone and we'll treat ourselves to an Amarone della Valpolicella 2010 ;-). Love and miss U!"

How deeply in love we are. After seven years, he instinctively knows when we have something special to celebrate. The small Italian place was the first restaurant we ever went to together, and we often go back. We have celebrated our first date, our first anniversary, our second anniversary, Rob's promotion, my father's death, Rob's next promotion and all our other anniversaries with a meal at that Italian restaurant.

I take the rest of the day off. There isn't much to do except boring paperwork and filing, anyway. The next stage of my career is now in the lap of the gods, whatever happens. With a kid, will I ever get promoted again? Or am I going to become one of the army of part-time moms, putting off my potential to a later date? I can't imagine doing any courses or training... I have to take things step by step, not get ahead of myself... my thoughts are in a whirl... I have to calm down, go home, and make myself pretty for Rob!

***

The little black dress? The long red one? Or more formal, with trousers and a blouse? ...I decide for a sexy look. My body is going to balloon over the coming months anyway, but I doubt I'll experience that

super-sexy phase. So I enjoy prettifying myself, for me and my husband. I squeeze myself into some Spanx, trying to get my rolls of fat tucked away so I can look okay in a clingy dress. I have never been one of those women with a super tight stomach, perky boobs and long, shapely legs. I'm more the short type, with skinny ankles, round ass, spare tire and breasts that sag a little if they aren't held up in a bra. Thankfully, my Arab roots on my mother's side give me a hint of the exotic. I have big, dark green eyes, black, curly hair that is often unruly, full lips, and light mocha skin.

In the shower, I use a lot of shower gel, I have to keep smelling good for a long time tonight. I stroke my belly and imagine how I'm going to look in just a few months, how my child will develop, and what a wonderful father Rob will be. He's Italian and he has always wanted to have a big family. Roberto Garreffa, from Rome, raised Catholic, and enormously passionate about everything he does. How is he going to react when I tell him in less than an hour that his dreams of a family are going to come true? I have to hold back my tears as I imagine it, otherwise my makeup will be spoiled... which may well happen later, but now I have to get going. I put on a coat and shoes and... the phone starts ringing... the telephone starts ringing? Who could it be, at this time of day? Nobody even knows I'm at home. The office would try to get me on my cell. Why ring on the landline? Strange, I wonder whether I should even pick up. I let it go to voicemail while I fasten my coat buttons and drape a scarf round my neck. There's a beep.

"You've reached Steiner and Garreffa. We could be anywhere, but we aren't home! Leave a message after the beep and we'll call you back!" *beep*

"Hello, Mrs. Steiner, it's Dr. Dubois, please call me as soon as you can on my emergency number, +41 79 922 25 28." He hangs up. My blood suddenly runs cold, my belly twists into a knot, and I go weak at the knees... My bag slips from my fingers as I stare in fear at the phone, almost as if it might be about to attack me.

CHAPTER 3

Dogs aren't allowed at the hospital so Frank has left Freja with his son. He quickly hurries across the underground parking garage to the lift. Why the hell is it called underground parking if it is a huge building alongside the main building? Or did Frank just mishear what the parking garage is really called? Obviously it should just be called the parking garage, but he is sure the nurse at reception in the ER said, "Please park in the underground parking garage, not outside the ER!" In fact she didn't say it, she yelled it right in his face. She most likely hadn't been having the best of days. He can't imagine what her and her colleagues must see at a big-city ER, day in, day out. What Frank has seen today is enough to last him a lifetime!

He hurries to the main entrance and is about to squeeze past a mass of people when he feels a hand on his shoulder that holds him back with a firm grip, "Frank? Frank Conley? Is that really you? Hey man, can I get a picture with you? I can't believe it! Frank Conley!" Before Frank can tear himself away from the stranger's grip he gets crushed between two men who stink of alcohol, stale cigarettes, and weed. Their fat, drunken fingers are fumbling to switch on selfie mode on their cell phones, then hold them out at shoulder height. Phone camera flashes, hoots of joy, a "Hey man, cool!" Frank manages to avoid the high fives as he makes his escape.

"Sorry guys, gotta go, have fun!" At the last moment, he lunges through the slowly closing doors into Coney Island Hospital, New York.

"Good evening, I'm Frank Conley, I was here before about the accident, can you tell me who I can speak to about it?" The woman behind the counter glances at Frank from behind her reading glasses while she slowly chews her gum. She casually takes off the glasses and lets them swing on their silver chain as she stands up and a wide grin spreads across her old but youthfully made-up face.

"Frank Conley, I could just die! Holy shit... sorry... what an honor, you at my counter, Sir! My god, you look even better in the flesh than in the papers or on the TV! Please excuse my language, I'm getting a little flustered!"

Frank closes his eyes for a fraction of a second, takes a deep breath, and replies calmly in his deep baritone voice, "I'm glad me being here is cheering you up. If I wasn't so beside myself because of the accident I would love to stay and talk longer. So can I ask you again to tell me who I can speak to about this? There was an accident this afternoon at Coney Island Beach."

The receptionist touches Frank's hand, which is resting on the counter. She puts her glasses back on her nose and winks at him as she settles back into her comfortable chair and her fingers go back to her keyboard. "Not just a pretty face," she says, "but a real gentleman, too! Let's go Susie, that's me by the way." She is already grinning and she winks again in Frank's direction. "Let's see if we can rustle up some information to put Frank's mind at rest. Ah, yes, here it is: intensive care unit 'A'. Are you a relative, Frank?" Susie looks at him above her glasses. Frank bites his lower lip and is about to answer, but Susie grabs a notepad, scribbles on it, places it on the counter and looks at Frank, again over her glasses. "Leslie, the skinny little white-haired lady in the blue skirt suit at the intensive care unit owes old Susie a coffee. She can bring it down to me when you get there. I'll just need an autograph!" Frank again feels Susie's brief, soft touch on his hand, which is now trembling as it picks up the piece of paper.

Frank manages to breathe out a barely audible, "THANK YOU Susie." Then he hurries to the elevator, which is empty, gets in and pushes the button for the fourth floor. His eyes close along with the doors and he whispers, "Oh god, let this nightmare be over! I want to be able to forget these images! Who would do something like this? It has to have been animals! No, beasts!" *ding* The door opens and Frank has the feeling he has arrived at an empty floor. Someone comes over, no, she floats over. The nurse's shoes must be made out of clouds. She glides past Frank, giving him a benign smile as she goes, then two seconds later she turns on her cloud and floats back before stopping right in front of him.

She smiles at him and asks softly, "Are you looking for anyone in particular?" Frank opens his shaking hand right in front of her face and lets Susie's note fall into the narrow, wiry hand of the woman on the cloud. She takes the small piece of paper, unfolds it as if it is a piece of cotton wool and reads Susie's handwriting. She slowly turns her cloud shoes in the direction of the cold, sterile and deathly silent corridor. She stands beside Frank, takes his arm almost tenderly and tells him in the same gentle voice, "I'll go with you, Leslie is just over there, by the drugs." She squeezes Frank's arm a little as she accompanies him in the direction of the medicine, and of Leslie. The place he hopes he will soon get all the answers to the most unbelievable questions of his life!

"Leslie," the floating woman says, "this gentleman has been sent by Susie." She smiles at him for the last time today as she glides out into the corridor. Leslie is a skinny, white-haired woman, just as Susie had described, and she gives Frank a confused look, her mouth puckered.

14

"This is intensive care. Who are you looking for?" She quietly closes the filing cabinet drawer that she has just placed a form in.

"There was an accident today," Frank whispers, hardly able to catch his breath, "on Coney Island Beach. I reported it. I followed the ambulance here but then I had to take my dog home. Can you tell me if the person that was brought here is okay?"

Leslie looks round, as if making sure nobody is there to overhear what she is about to say. "I'm sorry, I can't tell you anything unless you are a family member. I can see that Susie wants to do you a favor, for whatever reason, and I still owe her a coffee. She's like an elephant, she never forgets. So let me take you back to the elevator, and you can go back down to Susie." Frank's head slumps and he sighs in disappointment. Leslie takes him by the arm, just as the gliding lady had done before, making him wonder it if was part of their training, and takes him in the direction of the elevator. Frank glances at her, disappointed and confused. "Hey, I'm sure after all this excitement you want a glass of water, right?" she says sympathetically as she fills a cup with water from the cooler. Just then, a door opens and a doctor in a white coat appears in the doorway.

"Leslie, are you busy? I need a hand here." Leslie nods at Frank and turns to look at the doctor, who is still standing in the doorway.

"I'm not busy, I can help," she says, as she gives Frank the cup of water and goes over to the open door. The doctor has already gone back inside the room, and Leslie gives Frank a meaningful look as she follows. Frank knows what she is saying with that look. He quickly drinks one, two, three gulps from the cup and his hand, which had started to steady, begins to shake again. Behind this door, that is what she is telling him! The person involved in the accident from Coney Island beach is in the room behind this door.

While he is trying to work out how he can get more information, the curtain on the other side of the room's window is pulled open. Leslie is allowing him to see into the room, the entire room. The doctor opens the door again, and Frank hears him say to Leslie, "Keep this one under close observation. Keep checking the monitors, and make a note of the readings every 15 minutes. Call me if there is any change at all." He quickly hurries off along the corridor and disappears through another door. It is only now, as Frank watches him go, that he notices some of the curtains of the rooms are open. How did he miss that? He slowly empties the cup in loud gulps, drops it in the basket next to the cooler and now glides, just like the first lady he met, through intensive care to room INT7. Leslie looks at him through the glass and shrugs her shoulders doubtfully then slowly moves away from the bed to allow him to see the person lying there.

CHAPTER 4

Some Dadular Swiss magazines, including Vogue, are lying in front of me on the waiting room's coffee table like dead flies. I pour myself a glass of water and look down on the busy street. So many people hurrying to meetings, doing their shopping and catching the bus. Every one of them is carrying round their own personal destiny. I wonder if any of them are the same as mine? I can't imagine that they are, no I refuse to imagine it. I watch a young woman on the other side of the street as she gazes at the new collection from Swarovski. There is no way that she has any problems! Who would stop to look at jewelry if they had real problems? She has to be fine. And what about that man in a suit, looking through some documents as he waits for a tram. He looks annoyed, judging by the way he keeps

17

shaking his head. So the man has business problems? Can they really be so bad that they spoil his entire day? What am I saying, day! His life? It's just a job! It's not life and death! Worry about important things!

I'm suddenly ashamed about being angry at these two people! It's not their fault that my life has suddenly changed so drastically. I have a child inside me, the first living fruit of the love between Rob and me... or had? No it can't end this way! I can not accept it and I will not accept it. Why me? Why us? Why Rob? He would be such a great father and all I want is to be the mother of his child. I want to experience the ups and downs of family life with him, to get through them as our love grows stronger. Together! All three of us, or four, or five, or even six. Rob has always dreamed about a big table, surrounded by his offspring! All the children and grandchildren round a table! A house full of life, with joy and passion. Why in hell can't he have that, can't we have that? Why must the suffering come now, before we have even begun? What did we do wrong, to have this happen to us. Why wasn't I able to avoid this fate? Or was it more Rob's fate?

Dammit, when is Dr. Dubois going to come and get me, I can't stand these people and their carefree lives a second longer! Carefree or fake? Maybe they are just pretending everything is okay. Like in a play. Deep inside sad and dejected but on the surface the mask of perfection! I have never liked people like that. People are just people, so why not be true to your emotions and let it show when life does you wrong. Sure, it's not cool, but is that so important? Are you really soft if you allow yourself to have feelings, and to show them? Or is that what makes a strong personality, or at least makes you authentic! I never liked philosophy when I was at university, the ifs, ands and buts... simple facts, what actually happened, and obvious consequences were always easier to understand for me... but even these sometimes aren't enough. A person is incredible and exciting, but only if they dare to be a real person. Not a puppet on a string, not a gray fish in a stream, not a wannabe star, which means dying inside. Simply a person. Is that really so difficult?

"Mrs. Steiner, please." Dr. Dubois is standing at the entrance to the waiting room, face serious, as he motions me to follow him. Is this really what I want? Do I even want to go in there, to see my future, or a future I can't even imagine? I think seriously about opening the window and jumping down into the mass of people. I don't want to hear this, I don't want to see it! Can't the ground just open up and swallow me? A single thought flashes through my confused brain. Come on Jasmin, you have to pinch yourself, this has to be a nightmare, the worst nightmare of all time! Come on! Then you'll wake up, Rob is sleeping peacefully beside you and your joy will return! Not really believing it, I take the thought seriously enough to secretly pinch myself on the hip. "Mrs. Steiner, follow me please." Dr. Dubois gives me a very professional look. He knows exactly how close I am to losing my mind! He has known us for seven years, leading us through the jungle of medicine, spending even more time with us over the last four years as we tried for a family, and that dream has finally come true, but it could also be snuffed out in an instant.

"I'm sorry, I can't, please, I don't want to see that. I have to go, I want to go home!"

He is a very experienced doctor with a shock of white hair, big strong hands and a calm voice. He takes me by the hand and looks me in the eye, his gaze earnest but reassuring. His eyes tell me I have to get through this! "Come on, I'm here with you, we'll look at it together and then we'll talk it through afterwards. You don't have to do this alone, I'll help you!" he says, his words comforting me. I find his words very calming right now, so why do I just want to slap him? But I don't stop him as he leads me into the adjoining room.

CHAPTER 5

"Sir? Excuse me, Sir?" Frank is grabbed roughly by the arm.

He looks at the man in the white coat in confusion. "What?"

"I asked you if you are a relative of the victim?" the doctor asks, face serious, obviously not minded to tolerate any excuses.

"No, I'm not, I just wanted..." Frank hasn't finished his sentence before the tall doctor, though he is not as tall as Frank, escorts him by the arm to the elevator. But why in hell do they call it an elevator if it is about to bring Frank down?

"You are not allowed to be here if you aren't a family member. You should go to reception. They will be happy to help you to find the patient you're looking for." Before Frank knows what is happening, he's back in the same empty elevator as just five minutes before. Five minutes that have felt like an eternity to him, with images of earlier in the day going through his mind over and over. 'They'll be happy to help you...' Susie! He has to find Susie! She'll help him!

C'mon, c'mon, c'mon! Ding! Second floor! The door opens and a couple, obviously grieving, join Frank in the elevator. The woman has a Kleenex to her nose, but she can't hold back her tears. The man has his arm round her shoulders, obviously trying to be strong, to be a shoulder to cry on. But he too is unable to hide his grief. They nod to him and he nods in sympathy. Let's go, c'mon, Frank thinks, even though the grief in the elevator hangs as heavy as a dark cloud. At least his victim is alive! Victim! Yes, alive! Frank knows that, even though he couldn't see if it was a man or a woman, but his short-sighted, 58-year-old eyes could at least tell him that the victim was alive! The monitor beside the bed gave a regular beep, and he is no doctor but he guessed it must be a heartbeat. It was the constant beating of a heart, he is sure. There were lots of tubes, too, and that, along with the fact that the doctor said victim, and that they were still in a bed in intensive care, made him think the person was alive! The victim that Freja had found and he had identified as human, even if the sight was unimaginable!

Ding Ground floor. At last. Frank waits patiently for the grieving couple to leave the elevator, seemingly moving in slow motion, before hurrying by them, he has to get to Susie, right away. "Susie? Excuse me, Sir? Where's Susie?" Frank feels the blood draining from his face! This can't be happening. He is standing at reception, where Susie had been sitting with her reading glasses and mischievous smile, but now an older man with a mass of fair hair and a security guard uniform that is far too tight is sitting there.

"What was that?" he asks, obviously only now tearing his attention away from the game of solitaire he is playing on Susie's computer.

"I'm looking for Susie, the nice woman who was here at reception just now."

The man looks at Frank in astonishment, "Susie was just here? I took over from her over an hour ago, and she wanted to get home right away to tell her kids about an action hero, or something. No idea what's gotten into her today, I've never seen her leave in such a hurry. Maybe she came back because she forgot something?" Frank wonders who would put a man like this on a hospital front desk. What was his interview like? Hello, you are applying for a position on the security night shift. Do you have experience of gossiping? Do you like to sit down? Do you enjoy playing solitaire? Would you like to tell strangers about your life and ask inappropriate questions? Then you're exactly the person we're looking for! Congratulations, the job's yours. We don't have clothes in your size, but don't worry everyone looks good in a uniform!

Frank quickly forces these thoughts to one side and leans against Susie's counter as a shudder suddenly goes down his back... did he say an hour? He took over from Susie over an hour ago? Frank was in intensive care for over an hour? What was he doing for all that time? Was he looking at the victim for over an hour, watching the heartbeat on the monitor? "Can you tell me when Susie will be back?" The security guard seems miffed that Frank doesn't want his help.

"Why do you need her? Is there anything I can help you with?" he asks, seeming almost hurt. Frank tries to get out of the situation as gracefully as he can.

"I'm sure you can give me any information I want about the Coney Island Hospital. But Susie wanted something from me, and I promised I would get it for her. I didn't bring it with me today, I'm getting forgetful in my old age. I'd like to bring it to her tomorrow and I'd be much obliged if you would tell me when she'll be back, so I can surprise her with it when she starts her shift!" The solitaire-playing man softens.

"Getting old has its problems... I've been playing this game for months and I still haven't managed to get to the next level. Let me find the schedule and I'll tell you when you can surprise Susie! Is it something pretty?" His small eyes gaze at Frank, eager to hear about the gift. He has learned how to convincingly fake a coughing fit as an actor, and this skill saves him from continuing the ridiculous conversation, and solitaire man looks in a drawer for the time plan. Frank has to admit that at least this man is trying to help, and he is ashamed of having to lie to him. He silently congratulates the security guard on getting hired. "Ah yes, here it is, are you okay? Feeling better? Do you want a glass of water?" Frank shakes his head. "Oookkkkaaaay... Susie isn't here tomorrow, but she's back the day after. Her shift starts at nine. It looks like the lady will have to wait another day for her surprise. Or do you want to bring it in tomorrow, I can take it to her at home before my shift! She doesn't live far away. She comes in on foot, every day. That's what you call keeping fit, right? Although, you're very powerfully built, man!" Frank smiles tiredly at the man and pulls himself together one last time for this day.

"That's very kind of you! A very good idea! Or I could take it to her house myself! You know, I haven't seen those boys for a long time! What are their names again? ...damn... My old brain..."

"You mean Fred and John Jr? They're quite a pair, those two! They keep old Susie on her toes! But she's doing a good job with them! Suddenly having to raise two teenagers without a father, and working her fingers to the bone here, too, for the money we get! Hats off to her!"

"That's it! Fred and John Jr! I should surprise her at home, they'll get quite a kick out of it, do they still live in the same..." Frank is quickly trying to think of an address, when the telephone beside Susie's desk rings. Solitaire man lifts his index finger in front of Frank's face to tell him to wait a moment, and picks up. "Help desk! ... no, I'm sorry, Mrs.

Manders isn't here anymore... Yes... okay... I'd be happy to... bye." He puts the phone down, turns to Frank, but Frank has gone.

CHAPTER 6

We can do it! A mother and child can do anything, if they have to. Five percent! That's not nothing! Five percent chance of survival, that's what he said... I have to see the glass as half full, or even more than half, I will get through this ordeal!

What is five percent, anyway, when we are talking about life and death? I'd say it's everything! How dare Dr. Dubois be so pessimistic? Our whole family is now relying on JUST THESE five percent! It's not like I have any other option! I have always felt that settling scores by the odds will shake your confidence... even make you lose heart! I mean, if you prefer to believe in statistics from a text book rather than human willpower, the will to win or the ability to win, then good luck to you! And we are winners. We Steiners are winners! What would my father say, if he was still alive? He'd say, 'Sure, sure, these smart people with all their studies think they can explain their lives from books, instead of going out in the open air and looking at nature with all its wonders, where you can breathe in the meaning of life! See how many hours they waste studying, while true knowledge is waiting for them outside their door, as wonderful as your mother...' I miss my father. Right now, in this situation, he would take me by the hand, lay me on his chest and say, 'Jasmin, as long as you feel this pulse, you are alive! Don't waste time doing pointless things. Live!'

And how would Roberto react? He would also choose to see the bright side, even if it was only five percent. He would encourage me to get through with it, to fight for the three of us and be strong! Roberto, I'll do that for us! Sleep well habibi, it will all be okay! I gently stroke Roberto's cheek, his chin and kiss his lips. He looks so incredibly relaxed and carefree. His bright face on the white pillows looks like fine porcelain. I'm always asking myself how an Italian could have such fair skin. I wonder whether his family is really as pure blooded as they like to believe. But there is no arguing with Mama Garreffa. Questioning her or what she does would certainly mean war. And who wants that with their mother-in-law... or should it be 'mother-laying-down-the-law?' I'll be back soon habibi... I mean we will!

I leave the room, I have to get outside into the fresh air, to reality, to seek it, to gaze at it. The darkness strokes my face like a cool sea breeze... when this is all over, we have to go to the beach. We have always loved the seaside! Its many faces, all the aromas and its calm and wild sides. We love the surface of the sea and its depths. The sea is a guest at all our celebrations, or at least a visitor. If we go to New York, Paris or Barcelona instead of Sardinia, the Maldives or Mauritius, then we will at least have to visit the beach on the way back. It will all be over eventually, this whole damn nightmare.

I go a little way along the street, looking at all the lights in the windows, I hear the roar of the freeway in the distance and I follow the narrow gravel path to the creek. I hear it gurgling and think about the song my father once sang to us, Row, row, row your boat. Gently down the stream... a candle for a soul to be saved. I take three floating candles from my coat pocket and carefully light them, one after another, lay them gently on the slowly flowing stream and softly say a prayer. A prayer of supplication, a prayer of thanks, a prayer seeking help. A candle for every soul, a prayer for every heart that is still beating among our family that is not yet complete. I watch the candles float away, as my tears at last start to come!

I allow the tears to flow from my big dark eyes, I allow my lungs to draw in gasps of air to accompany even more of my tears! I want to scream my heart out, and the pain with it, the horror of my situation has hit me so hard. I want to get to the lowest point of my whirl of thoughts, and I want to get there here and now, so I can be re-energized for what is to come. During my training I have often came across articles about how when you reach your lowest point, that's when things really start to improve. I must have hit rock bottom today, today I have to find the strength to bring the three of us through the hell that might be coming our way. Wait, stop, don't tempt fate by saying hell. My mother said, 'We can have paradise on earth!' I want paradise, and I want to live in it with Roberto and our children!

I can't see the candles any more for tears. I wipe them away and notice how puffy my eyes feel. I see the tiny flickering flames floating away, say goodbye to my lowest point and make my way back to Roberto, back to paradise.

CHAPTER 7

"Where is your car, sir?" three men in uniform are standing in front of Frank.

"Sorry?" Frank understood the words of the question, just not the meaning.

"Your car, where did you park it, sir?" the question is repeated. Frank again stares incredulous. The police officers take a step nearer to Frank's frozen form. "Is everything okay, sir? Would you like to go back inside and see a doctor? You seem very confused. Do you feel unwell? Do you want to sit down?" Frank nods at the mention of somewhere to sit down, and notices a row of seats near the entrance. He sits, supporting himself with his elbows on his lap, rubbing his exhausted eyes which have seen unimaginable things today. The three officers stand near him, unhurriedly giving him a moment to collect himself. He thinks he recognizes the face of the man in uniform. He has spoken to this man before, but when? Where? And why? He suddenly feels ill, only just having time to lean to the side and vomiting up the entire contents of his stomach onto the damp ground. He heaves again and again before at last thankfully taking a Kleenex from one of the officers to wipe his mouth.

"I'm sorry, it's all been too much today. What did you ask me again? Did you really mean me?" One of the officers sits next to Frank, puts his hand on his shoulder and gives him a friendly, consoling pat.

"Mr. Conley, I'm sorry about what you have been through today, and I can imagine how you feel. The reality is much worse and much uglier than in films. Do you have family at home, or somebody we can take you to? You shouldn't be alone today. The things you've seen will stay with you for a while." Frank gets the feeling that throwing up has broken the spell of stupor, the trance, his missing hour. Officer Tropman! He asked him questions for a whole hour in the waiting room in intensive care. He had been treated like a suspect, the man questioning him about every moment. He had interpreted every gesture as a guilty plea. It was an hour when he had to explain over and over what he had really been doing on the beach. Where is the dog now? Why did he go to Coney Island Beach when he lived in the Hamptons? How did he get to the intensive care unit, and how did he know exactly which room the victim was in? Officer Tropman, the man who has made today even worse than it already was, and who almost made Frank wonder if he was guilty. What an arrogant dick, and now he was patting him on the shoulder, as if they had been friends for years, imparting words of wisdom.

Frank stands up, concentrates on staying on his feet, tosses the Kleenex in the waste basket next to the bench that the officer who wants to be his new friend is getting up from. "Thank you for your offer, but I'm feeling okay. I'll go get my car, and I can get home by myself. Like I said, I'll call you if I remember anything else, of if I have any questions. You get in touch with me if you have any other questions, and I will not leave the country, but if I have to because of my job I will notify you immediately." He nods at the officers and confidently strides in the direction of the parking garage, AKA the underground parking. No police officer was going to drive his car, his Aston Martin with all the optional extras that had been imported specially for him from Europe. This arrogant dick certainly didn't deserve that, in fact it was the last thing he wanted at the end of this shitty day!

"My god, Dad! What is going on, what was all that about, earlier today? Is everything okay with you? Are you all right?" The worried questions of his son fill the car on a hands-free call. Frank drives out of the garage and heads home, seeing the Coney Island Hospital in his rear-view mirror for the last time that day.

"I'm fine, everything's okay. Kenneth, I'm sorry, I didn't want to worry you but I had to find somewhere for Freja as quickly as possible. How is she?"

"She's upset, she's really not herself. What happened? I couldn't even get her to come out for a jog with me. Where are you? Are you on your way here?"

"I've had a shitty evening, and I don't want to go over the whole thing again. I hope you understand. I promise I'm okay! There was an accident on the beach, Freja found an injured person, and I wanted to go to the hospital and find out if they were okay. That's the short version. Can I leave her with you for tonight? I just want to go home, throw myself under the shower then hit the hay."

"Yeah, sure. I'll look after her. If you need anything, just give me a call, okay? I'll see you tomorrow, okay?"

"Okay, see you tomorrow. Thanks son!" A good boy. Frank was very proud of him. Despite the loss of his mother in a tragic accident when he was a kid, he has turned out well. His drive and his strong will have ensured he has lived an exciting life. After college, he studied at NYU School of Law and he has a Masters and his Ph.D. He is now Dr. Kenneth Conley after becoming a law professor at his university. He loves the university and is proud of having gone to the same institution as John F. Kennedy Jr. 'Who knows, Dad, maybe I'll be president one day! Anything's possible if you just want it bad enough and work for it!' Frank has to chuckle whenever Ken dreams out loud. Barbie's boyfriend in the White House! Ken really does look a little like the legendary children's toy. He is athletic, without having to exercise much, he is 6'2", dark brown hair, which he keeps in a neat but young style, blue eyes from his mother and a deep and comforting voice. Frank idly wonders if anyone has ever heard Barbie's actual boyfriend speak, as he dials 411 on his Blackberry.

"411, this is Gaby, how can I help you?"

"Gaby, I need the address of Susan Manders in Coney Island, please." He hears the clatter of keys over the line, Gaby's breathing, and then her voice fills the Aston Martin.

"Susan Manders, 36 Brighton 10 Terrace. Would you like me to send you the address as a text message?"

"Yes, thanks very much, Gaby!"

"Any time, sir. Have a wonderful night in New York!" Gaby has only just hung up when his Blackberry hums and Susie's address appears on the screen.

"What the hell...!" Frank curses to himself, as he drives up to his gate. Cameras flash as at least ten reporters yell questions at him and point microphones.

"Frank Conley, are you involved in a brutal murder? Do you know the victim? Did you see the murderer?" Frank pushes the button on the remote that opens the gate. Floodlights come on as well, confusing the pack of reporters and allowing him to hit the gas, allowing his tail lights to disappear behind the already closing gate. How in hell did they find out already? Who was the one who leaked this to them? No, it can't be her. Not Susie, she seems so helpful and obliging, not like somebody who would use information for their own advantage, or for a few minutes of fame. Instead, all his anger focuses on the arrogant dick of a police officer. Officer Tropman. Frank makes sure to remember his name, he is not finished with that man.

Frank doesn't care much, or even at all, about the intrusive questions and stupid ideas of the gutter press, it is the word 'murder' that has confused him and made him think. If Officer Tropman is the leak, he might have told the press more about the victim than Frank has been told, including details like background and medical condition. Has the victim died? Was it animals that did this, or could it have been people? If it was animals, why would they be saying it was murder?

Frank is mad at himself for even listening to the stupid questions of the reporters at his gate... and yet, even after a hot shower, a juicy steak, and a generous glass of 188-year-old Highland Park, he still can't get to sleep.

CHAPTER 8

Just four weeks have passed since I left Dr. Dubois with a heavy heart and much trepidation. Weeks of brutal and naked reality, weeks of battling with myself, my mind, my sanity, outbursts of emotion, moments of sadness and joy, love and security. And now another important milestone, her first trimester tests. At 36, any pregnancy is already risky. Those statistics again!

It is the likely outcome that determines what our attitude to our pregnancy is going to be. We see how many people give birth to a healthy baby after the age of 35, with no complications, and we worry. But in my situation, this statistic is suddenly of the least importance. My age isn't the most important factor anymore, considering what the doctors just found during their tests, in their laboratories. I wonder how the tests are even carried out? Hundreds of test tubes of blood with names on, or maybe just numbers? Behind every number a person with a heart, a body, and soul. Tests using cutting-edge machines, punching data into a new computer, developed by the best minds, then some calculations are done and voila! Your results come and you have been sentenced to death! A new label is put on the tube, from a bunch of identical ones spat out by a printer, then it's put in an envelope and sent back to the specialist who then has to give the bad news. What do these lab rats do next? Go for lunch in the canteen to chat with colleagues? How many tubes have you processed today? Did you find anything interesting? Are you getting on okay with the new software? Do you print the results in color, or black and white? They told us that we're supposed to save paper. Man, this new latte macchiato here is delicious, they even provide you with different flavors! What kind of person takes a job like that? I wonder if, as part of their training, they should be with the specialist when their report is passed on to the patient, to see the effects.

"Mrs. Steiner please." Dr. Dubois is, as always, in his white coat, and as usual points to THE room, which has been a torture chamber in my mind. But not today, I'm sure of that! Today it will be a place of joy! Roberto gives my hand a happy squeeze and can hardly wait to follow Dr. Dubois into the room. "Mr. Garretta, it's a pleasure to see you again! How are things at the clinic?" Dr. Dubois motions Roberto to one of the empty chairs in front of his desk, then he shakes my hand. He holds it tight and gives me a meaningful look and an encouraging nod. His gaze assures me that he will go along with our arrangement, and I sit in the remaining empty chair.

"Not bad, it's a nice team, and people are nicer in a private clinic. Things are run differently here, I can see that. I haven't seen you in a long time, do you usually operate somewhere else?" Dr. Dubois opens my file, flips through a few pages, lost in thought.

"I move from clinic to clinic," he says, almost casually, "depending on what the patient wants and the equipment I need. But tell me how you are, Mrs. Steiner?" He gives me an appraising look and I try to answer calmly.

"I feel good. I don't feel as sick as I did at the beginning, my breasts are a little sore and I get out of breath quickly when I go upstairs or do exercise."

"Your breasts are sore? On a scale of zero to ten, how painful is the soreness?"

I remember his promise and I say, still calmly. "It's nothing, really, just a little, now and again. Can we see what the baby looks like, and hear the heartbeat?" I'm trying to move things along. Dr. Dubois hits the desk very gently with his fist and nods.

"Then let's get you on the couch." In the next room he has the chair that must be the favorite of every woman, with two helpful metal attachments for the legs and an examination table beside it. In between is the mobile monitor that Dr. Dubois calls his Rolls Royce, because he hasn't had it long and he can see things he has never seen before, in 3D. I lie on the couch and lift my blouse to just below my bra. Dr. Dubois spreads ice-cold gel over my stomach and picks up the magic eye of the monitor, which he moves across my stomach. And there it is! Clear as day, our baby!

My heart beats faster and I grin at Roberto. He stares at the monitor, frozen in place, as tears fill his eyes. He quickly wipes them away, not wanting to miss a second of what he can see on the monitor. Dr. Dubois nods in satisfaction, constantly changing the angle of view presented on the monitor. Then he turns the large knob that turns up the volume, and it sounds like a galloping horse. He zooms in on the outline of the baby and we see the wildly beating heart! Our child's heart! I can not hold back my tears of joy, and I reach for Roberto's hand. He is shaking and I look him in the eye, I see how much he already loves our child.

"Everything looks good, circumference of the head, length, nuchal fold thickness, all good! You have a lively baby!" The head of the baby keeps moving, it looks like it is doing somersaults. It is really turning, round and round, and we both have to laugh! Dr. Dubois takes a still photograph and presses the button to print. He takes the magic eye from my stomach and wipes the remains of the gel from my skin. My husband and I feel a brief moment of disappointment, what a pity. We could have watched our tiny athlete work out for hours. I wonder if it is possible to buy a device like this for our house?

***

On cloud nine, we go out into the busy street hand in hand. None of these people interest me today, all I care about is our happiness. How egotistical a person can be, I suddenly don't care if somebody has a worse fate than mine, or if somebody is worried about things that don't matter. My only thoughts are about the wonderful little life growing within me. Six and a half centimeters long already, how is that possible? And a wonderful heartbeat, a melody that will accompany me the entire day.

"Honey, I have to get going. I would prefer to stay here with you, but I have to do an operation later today." Honey... Roberto hasn't called me that in a long time. It shows me how happy he is to be living a full life again. I pray that I won't have to suddenly take this joy away from him. I quickly push these unwelcome thoughts away and put my arm round his athletic body. My face just comes up to chest height. He hugs me tight, kisses my head and lets go of me so he can kiss me lovingly on the mouth. "I love you both and missing you already, see you this evening. Take care and don't let school get to you. I won't be late, I'll be home at seven at the latest, okay?" I nod contentedly. "I hope the operation goes well, and be nice to the bosses!" I wink at him and we go off in different directions.

CHAPTER 9

Susie stands there, mouth open, curlers in her hair, wearing a cream color bathrobe and gold slippers with rhinestones, in the open door of her simple house on Coney Island. "I'll be damned, I don't believe it! What are you doing here? Holy shit, what must I look like? And what do you look like? Are you feeling all right?" Susie's refreshing manner enchants Frank, and a smile appears on his face, which he is trying to hide beneath a baseball cap, with his collar pulled up.

"You look great, Susie! Can I come in?" Frank sees the unease in her eyes. Despite that, she steps back and allows him in. She shoots an appraising look at the street and closes the door behind them. Frank finds himself in a small living room with a comfortable atmosphere. He looks around and feels bad for the way ordinary people live. Susie seems to read his thoughts.

"Do you want to move in here," she asks, "to get a taste of how ordinary people live. I bet you only know places like this from the studio." She raises an eyebrow and goes to the open-plan kitchen, stopping behind an old wood counter with a lot of framed photos.

"It's very cozy here, may I?" Frank picks up a frame to look at the photo within.

"Make yourself at home. When you're ready, can I ask you why you're here? I'm guessing it's not because you fell in love with me at first site yesterday." She takes two cups from a wood cupboard and pours in some fresh coffee. "Sugar, sweetener, milk?"

"Black, please."

"Is that the secret to your good looks? I should try that, but it tastes awful!" Susie gives Frank his cup and joins him in looking at the framed photograph. "We were all still together then," she explains. "My kids, Fred and John Jr, and

John Sr. He passed away three months ago. Lung cancer. He used to smoke like there was no tomorrow. Then he was gone. That asshole. Just left us here in this place, just because he lost the will to go on. The kids really miss him, that SOB. But who am I talking to about the rage that gets left behind when you lose somebody, you lost your wife too..." She sips at her coffee and goes to an easy chair with a pretty crocheted blanket on it. She drops down into it and smooths the blanket on the back. "Okay, sexy, spit it out, why are you here?"

"Please, call me Frank." He sits opposite her on the salmon color sofa, which is actually very comfortable. He decides he should also get some comfortable furniture, as he throws one leg casually over the other. "Susie, I really want to thank you for all your help yesterday. I would never have found the right room without you." At last Susie smiles.

"It was my pleasure, Frank. Sometimes the rules can be bent a little. If I learned anything from my late husband, it's that sometimes the rules have to be broken if you want to help people. I could tell how desperate you were yesterday, and boy, did you look damn good..." Susie grins, winks at Frank and takes a sip of her coffee.

"To be honest, Susie, that's not the only reason I'm here... I wanted to... to ask you..."

Susie puts her cup on the wobbly coffee table and slaps her hand on her thigh. "Frank, this isn't going to turn into an embarrassing proposal of marriage, not with me in this outfit and curlers in my hair! There's no reason to look at me that way, I haven't lost my mind, my mind's pretty good in fact! Now let's stop this charade about you being here just to say hello. What is going on, you want more information, right? They threw you out of intensive care because you aren't family."

Frank relaxes into Susie's sofa and thinks about how great this woman is. How down to earth and natural she is. He imagines it would be a lot of fun to spend an evening with her. Perhaps they would do just that when the business in the hospital was over. "You got it in one. You seem to have a lot of experience, or am I just easier to read than I thought." Frank finishes his coffee. "Good coffee, by the way. Colombian?" He has hardly spoken the words when he bites his lip and wishes the sofa would just swallow him up.

"Sure, sure, Columbia, but in my world it's called W-a-l-m-a-r-t," she draws out the word as if speaking to a person with impaired hearing. "It's okay Frankie, don't worry about it. I can take it. If I shit in a golden toilet like you, I would want to keep it secret, too!" She laughs and gets up to get Frank's cup. "Can't decide? Want another taste of Colombia, sugar cube?" Frank nods thankfully and follows her into the kitchen.

"What do you think, is there any way you can help me? I know I'm asking a lot, and I don't want you to jeopardize your job, but I would be happy to pay for..." C'mon Frank, not again! Just as he is expecting, he has to take a couple of steps back to escape her furious face.

"Okay, that's enough! Do I look like I can be bought? Like I wouldn't do anything just from the goodness of my heart? Like I need to take your money? Come on. If you really want anything from me, you need to switch on the brain in that pretty head and work your trained butt off! You can't speak that way to me, understand?"

"I'm sorry, Susie, please, I take it back, I just wanted..."

"All right, drink your black coffee and let mom do her thing!" She gives him the full mug of delicious Walmart coffee and goes back into the living room. She picks up the telephone, sits in her chair and dials a number. "Hey Leslie, it's Susie... yeah that's right, it's my day off, is everything okay there with you? ...No way? With the blonde bitch from number two? He's nuts, he'll go off with anybody. Say, what was that about an accident on the beach yesterday? Did somebody get into trouble? They're saying on the news...aha...hm...er...um. What the hell!!!" Susie holds her hand over her mouth, shocked, tears of horror coming to her eyes. "Who would do something like that? Dammit Leslie, how do you stand it? What's going to happen? Will she live?" Frank comes upright on the sofa, he interlaces his fingers, hardly able to sit still. His breath comes quick and shallow, his heart beats fast and loud! She! It's a woman. And what was that about the news? Have the vultures outside his house put something together and broadcast it? He is going to have to ring Tom. His manager is going to be furious with him if he hears on the news before Frank tells him. He impatiently forces himself to try and concentrate on what Susie is saying into the phone. She wipes the tears from her eyes but the shock is still written all over her face. "What do you mean... no family? I don't understand. Somebody must miss her! Aha... okay, sure... 24 hours, you say... holy shit, can you imagine, how somebody is going to react to that. I mean, the kid has to have a father! What?

48

Okay, I get it, don't worry about it hon, thank you! See you tomorrow, I'll bring coffee and donuts!" Susie hangs up, while Frank is surprised that telephones like this are still in use. Who is it, a woman, a child? A young girl? Susie looks at Frank and shakes her head. "Would you like a whiskey? I know I could use one. Frank Conley, you have landed our hospital with quite something, that's for sure..." For the first time Frank sees not just dismay, but worry on Susie's face.

CHAPTER 10

The moment of truth has come. I have to tell the director of my college about the pregnancy. Apart from my full breasts and the acne that I have had since the beginning of the pregnancy, there hasn't been much change. I use loose clothes to hide the bump, but things are progressing quickly, and now I want my friends and the whole world to hear my good news!

I want to go shopping for the baby, and start a yoga course for pregnant women. None of that would be possible without the school finding out. Especially not Claudia. She is the best assistant ever, but also the nosiest person in the school. Maybe that's why she's so good. She knows everything about everybody. I'm the head of Teaching and Art, and there is nothing in the way of me becoming principal. Could that turn into a part time job, and what is the situation with maternity leave? The thought of remaining head of the department forever because I'm becoming a mom makes me shiver. I wonder if I should give up the job to become a mother and a housewife? With Roberto's salary as an operating room assistant at a private clinic, it would certainly be possible, but would that be enough for me? Would I be happy? Would there be enough variety and challenge in my life? When you think how long many women study and do further education, only to hang up their qualifications and professional skills in order to be a mother... All the money for all that study, wasted... Who can say if these women are really happier, or even happy enough. I'm sure there are plenty of statistics and scientific studies, especially in women's magazines. Who knows, maybe I'll buy one today.

"Jasmin, I hope everything is alright and you haven't had a fight with one of the other department heads. You know, your reputation is MORE important to your career than your qualifications!", exclaims the director of our college, Dr. Martin Kunz, who is actually a good boss. Very approachable, very down to earth, despite his outstanding qualifications and skills. He is a very Dadular man, even gives some lectures himself to the older students, and is often asked for an opinion by news channels. An astonishing career for someone who has just turned 50! He has two children and, after the birth of the first daughter, his wife now stays home with the children full time. She was a teacher at the college too. I wonder if her giving up her career drove him onward twice as fast?

"Yes, everything's fine," I answer and sit on a chair in his office. He also sits and crosses his legs before looking at me expectantly.

"I wanted to ask you about the position as principal. Would it be possible to do the job part time?" Jasmin, Jasmin, Jasmin, never getting to the point...

"I don't understand, do you want to reduce your hours?" He looks at me in astonishment.

"Hm, well, perhaps," I stammer. You've lost your cool, Jasmin! Pull yourself together! You are getting all you've ever wanted! This here, is just a job! "The truth is, I'm pregnant. Four months." I hardly dare look him in the eye, and I'm taken completely by surprise when he jumps up and comes over to me.

"That's great news! Congratulations!" He embraces me, and I'm so in shock I can't move. Professor Kunz is embracing me! "I'm so happy for you and Roberto! Four months, you say? Okay, let me work it out, that means the due date is in July or August, right?" Only a father would speak like this, I think, which reassures and relaxes me. The die is cast, and wheels seem to be in motion.

Loaded down with shopping, I hurry through the streets to our loft. It is a big place, and a very harmonious place to live. It has two floors with lots of wood and open galleries, a nice little kitchen and floor-to-ceiling windows that look out over the whole city. There is also a terrace from which you can see most of the lake in summer. We were very lucky to get it, you don't see many like it come up for sale on the Internet. These types of flats are usually found via word of mouth. Roberto's predecessor on the operating room team had lived here with his partner.

Unfortunately, they broke up after ten years together. It was a real shame, they had seemed so good together and were such nice people. After the breakup, he went to work abroad in a hospital in New York, and never came back. We have wanted to go see Simon for a long time, and it's surprising how quickly two years, or more, have passed. Roberto often speaks to him on the phone, and Simon has been back a few times to deal with paperwork. It is very different working over there. Roberto is always fascinated by his stories of living there and working at an American hospital. We'll have to see if we can get a flight before the seventh month, after that I've read I won't be allowed to fly. I'll ask Roberto today, I think it would be a wonderful choice for our last trip as just the two of us. It will be a long time before we get to have a holiday in a big city after that, no doubt.

I schlep the heavy bags up to the fourth floor, the wood creaking beneath my feet. The disadvantage of living in this beautiful old building is that there is no elevator. I can already hear the beautiful sound of our piano. Roberto's fingers glide over the keys. 'Fuer Elise' ...our song. So simple and yet so touching. It was the song for my music exam when I graduated from school and, it turns out, the first song he learned to read from sheet music. We play it for each other, as if we need to keep practicing it. Technically it isn't difficult to play, but it's a lot of fun and you can vary the song to suit your mood.

Roberto takes his hands from the keyboard when he hears the doorknob. "No. Keep playing!" I yell into the living room as I take off my coat and shoes, take the bags into the kitchen, then go over to Roberto at the piano. I run my fingers through his hair and put my arms round his shoulders. I sway with him as he moves along the keys, breathing in his aroma, feeling his warmth and allowing his calm to seep into me. What a cozy and warm feeling. I wish moments like this would last forever.

Anyone who has never been in love has really missed out on an important part of life. It's such a shame that not everyone has the right person for them. Or maybe the person does exist, but they just can't find them? Whatever, I'm just glad I found the person who completes me! "We should visit Simon," I whisper into his ear. Roberto plays to the end of the piece, and keeps his foot on the pedal to allow the last note to linger.

"It's funny you should say that. He crossed my mind a few times today, and I had the same thought! How long before you won't be able to fly? Will you need a note from your doctor?" I let go of his warm body and go to the kitchen, to unpack the bags

"I'll ring Dr. Dubois tomorrow and find out all about it." I take an apple from one of the bags and playfully throw it to Roberto. "Let's go to the Big Apple!"

CHAPTER 11

"Hey Tom, yeah, I'm fine. What are they saying on the news? ...No, no murder... damn vultures... nothing like that, all exaggeration, as usual. I was on Coney Island beach with Freja... why not? I wanted to go see Ken, get a change of scenery. I hadn't been to Coney Island in a long time, and it's not far from him... so what, I can go jogging wherever I want. It was bad enough that police officer looking funny at me because of it... yeah the police interviewed me... just listen, okay?" Frank is sitting on the back seat of his Mercedes-Maybach, telling Tom, his good friend and manager, about what has been happening over the previous 24 hours. "And, you know what? I want a telephone. A real one with a receiver I can hang up. ...buttons or dial, I don't care... yes in the bedroom, next to the bed... what? So get a line put in... remind me, what's the name of that interior designer? ..That's right, Silvia, tell her I want a comfortable sofa... no, that's not a sofa, it's some kind of leather bench, and it is not comfortable. I want a sofa that's really cozy... okay? ...I don't know, either, but I think I just want to feel human again... this whole thing is weighing on my mind. I keep seeing it all before my eyes, her lying there, whimpering... how many people have died in my movies? How many people have I killed? ...and now I've seen somebody near death, for real, and I can't get it out of my head... dammit Tom, I think it's time I started doing something else... different kinds of films... I have to do some good..." Frank puts his Blackberry down and stares out the window, lost in thought. His driver is taking him through the heavy traffic in the direction of Brooklyn.

Freja jumps up at Frank almost the second Ken opens the door. "Okay, hell... it's okay, let me in..." Frank has to force his way through the door to get into Ken's apartment. Then follows a fatherly embrace, with few words spoken, a slap on the back and Freja circling the two of them.

"Is everything okay, dad?" Ken gives him a concerned look with his twinkling blue eyes. "Do you want something to drink?" He goes to the open-plan kitchen of his two-storey apartment and grabs a 7 Up from the refrigerator. He opens the can on the way back to Frank, who sits down in a checkered wing back chair.

"Thanks son, I'm doing a lot better. I'm starting to be able to deal with all this. It's not actually about me..." and for the second time that day, he talks about exactly what happened on the beach and at the hospital. What he doesn't say, either time, is anything about his visit to Susie. He can't explain why, but he somehow has the feeling he should keep that to himself.

"What are you going to do now? What happens next? Can I do anything? I can only imagine what will happen to the guy or guys who did this horrendous thing. Crimes like this are punished severely... if they ever catch them. Pieces of shit like that know what they're doing, and they're often very clever. It was no coincidence, it had to be planned. Poor woman! She's been through hell, and the worst is yet to come! I wonder if she'll even survive? Tell me, how did you find out about her condition?"

That was the difference between his manager and his lawyer son, always questioning, always the sly fox. How proud he was of the boy! "That doesn't matter right now, let's just say, your Dad has a source." He winks at Ken, scratches Freja behind the ear and takes a big gulp from the can. "I just want to think about something else, just wear myself out on the tennis court. I'm not going to get any more information today. Maybe I'll go to the hospital tomorrow. What do you think? Do you want to give your old dad a game?" Ken looks through he window at the street, his lips pursed in thought the way his mother's always used to when she was thinking.

"I'd love to..." he then says, "and I've got time... but there's something else I'd like to do with you dad... and today seems to be the right time for it..."

CHAPTER 12

"Have you spoken to Roberto? I think it's important he knows all the facts. When things get tough, he has to know what his decision is going to be." Dr. Dubois gives me a worried but critical look.

"No, I haven't found the right moment. But I know he would have made exactly the same choice. Except it's my body. And our child. So, I have to make the right decision for both of us, right? I'll keep to our extra appointments, and come for regular checkups, and have the extra tests your

lab rats need." He gives me a skeptical look and, of course, he doesn't know what destructive thoughts have been going through my mind. "I have another question. What week is the latest I can take a long-haul flight?"

Dr. Dubois drops his pencil and his concerned expression is now mixed with shock. "You aren't telling me you want to fly? In your condition? What are you going to do if something happens? Where do you want to go, for god's sake?"

I have never wondered whether doctors even believe in God. Isn't there a contradiction between medical facts and biblical miracles? An interesting theory, I'll have to go to the library and see if there are any good books about it. I'm pretty sure that there must be a published theologian who initially decided for medicine and then changed their mind, believing in miracles after all. "Mrs. Steiner, where do you want to go?" My favorite gynecologist doesn't have it easy with me. I wonder if I'm the only patient of his right now who he thinks is certifiably insane.

"Sorry, to New York. And I'm sure that, if something happens, I'll be in good hands there. We're visiting a friend who is an operating room assistant, too. So, I'll have an inside track, if you know what I mean! So, what's the answer? How long will the airlines allow me to fly?" Dissatisfied with my reply, he flips through his calendar.

"You are now in the fifteenth week. Most airlines will allow you to fly until the thirty-second week, if you have a note from your doctor. Unfortunately, I won't be able to give you one. I could only do that if your pregnancy was going well and there was no risk." His gaze falls on me, and I can hardly stand it!

"I understand, but surely I can travel up to the twenty-fifth week without a doctor's note?" I ask him, though I am determined that I will not allow him to change my mind.

"Listen, Jasmin, I don't want to overstep the mark, but we aren't haggling over your life or that of your child. I can't condone that you are neither telling your husband, the father, what the real situation is with you and your child, nor that you could be risking the lives of all three, or create a very difficult situation for Roberto. What makes you think this is all so simple? You have to be sensible about this, you understand?" Dr, Dubois is now really furious and it makes me feel really sorry that I'm such a disappointment to this overqualified and unbelievably likable and sympathetic doctor. But I don't feel ashamed at all about my behavior, and I try to explain myself.

"Dr. Dubois," I say, gently, "I've been your patient for years and I trust you completely. We've been trying to have a child for over four years, and there didn't seem to be anything physically wrong, but it just never happened. It was a miracle that I suddenly got pregnant, and both our wishes, Roberto's especially, were granted. Then, at pretty much the same time, your revelation of my life-threatening circumstances, which shouldn't make any difference! But it's true, I should have decided immediately, either for me or the child we have been yearning for so long. But, after deciding against the innocent young life, nobody would be able to assure me I could carry a child again. You know what I was thinking from the moment I had to make this decision? To hell with it? Yeah! I'm sorry to have to use such harsh language, but I am still completely convinced I have made the right decision. I've decided that we will both make it through alive! Both of us, for Roberto and our family!"

This short outburst, quite uncharacteristic for me, has left me breathing heavily, and I slump back against the chair. Dr. Dubois looks blindsided and gives me a sad look from behind his glasses.

"Try to go before the end of your twenty-fifth week. I want you to come and see me again before you leave, that's my last request to you." I nod understandingly and I think, I have the best gynecologist in the world. I put on my coat, after booking my next appointment for four weeks time, where I will bring Rob for 'baby watching'. Dr. Dubois sticks his head out of his door and asks, "Mrs Steiner, just for my notes, which hospital does your friend work at?"

"Coney Island Hospital, New York," I tell him, with a smile of thanks.

Chapter 13

It was a great trip and Kenneth was right, it was somehow the right time. For a lawyer, he's too sensitive, Frank thinks, and once again feels a surge of pride over his son. It is unclear to him why, for whatever reason, he hasn't had a serious, meaning long-term, relationship. Of course, his work is important to him, but his son isn't the kind of career-focused person who doesn't care about human relationships. Quite the opposite, even during his time at university, seeing his father was always important to him, as well as his grandparents and also his college buddies. He has always been a people person, who would chat to a hot dog vendor, or become interested in a book being read by somebody on the subway. Ken has been interested in people since he was young. People, who they are, how they think and of course justice. He was always very good at dealing with his father being in the limelight and being so often in the public eye. He was quite proud of his father when the guys at his university spoke enthusiastically about Frank's films. But he realized this was just his father's job, and he didn't try to use it to his advantage. He often liked to keep the identity of his famous father secret, so as not to be seen as his son, but to allow people to get to know him as his own person. They had a lot of arguments about his roles. Frank, the action hero who killed people in his films and did all kinds of illegal things, it was against all his son's instincts of logic and justice. They often agreed that artistic freedom and imagination, no matter how horrific and unintelligible, even illogical, had to remain almost unlimited. He often didn't tell people his father was an actor, no, he simply called him an artist.

The golden age of this artist has given him many moments of luxury, such as this evening, allowing him to escape the present. They were flying in a small private jet to the house in the country, which he didn't have as much chance to use as he would like, to visit Ken's mother's nearby grave. The grave of Frank's wife. It was always beautifully decorated with seasonal foliage, and the white, marble headstone with a dove gave it a sense of dignity. "Do you still love her, Dad?" Ken's tearful eyes rest on the dove. Frank steps closer and puts his arm round him.

"I will always love her, and have her in my heart. She was the love of my life, and that doesn't change just because she is dead. What's wrong?"

Ken wipes his tears away with a movement of his hand, and replies, "I often think about her, even if I didn't get to spend many years with her. It sometimes feels like she's with me, sounds strange doesn't it? I can't cling on to these memories too hard, because then the pain comes and I don't know how to deal with it. Do you know that feeling?"

"Yes, I know it very well. It hurts, a lot, when you really miss somebody, and you want to say so much to them, hold them in your arms, or do things together. That's okay, it's a normal part of life. But I don't have an exact recipe for getting rid of the pain any quicker. I have noticed how it does me a lot of good to talk about it, to share. And you know I'm here for you, whenever you need me! Maybe it would help if you were seeing somebody." Frank gently nudges him in the side, and he notices that Ken has taken what he is saying on board, but is making a show of ignoring it.

They eat something at the diner in town, to the pleased surprise of the owner, who hasn't seen them in a long time. At home, they look through old photo albums together, smile and become lost in their memories. They silently share their pain.

On the return journey, Frank's cell hums in his waistcoat pocket, but he doesn't want to spoil the time he is sharing with his son for anybody. Whoever it is, if it is important they'll ring again. It is already late when Frank finally gets home to the Hamptons. At least the vultures from the news have gone. They must have found somebody even juicier than him to sink their teeth into. Freja runs to her bowl, cracks a couple of dog treats in her jaws and laps at her water before settling down in her basket, exhausted. Frank is tired too, and he takes off his clothes, wraps a towel round his hips and switches on his sauna. He goes into the kitchen to get a bottle of water with lemon. His cell hums again, a number he doesn't recognize. He checks the number from earlier and sees that it is always the same number. Ten calls! Who could it be? Frank checks the number on the police officer's business card. When he sees the name, Daniel Tropman, he raises an eyebrow. He remembers, he has a bone to pick with this man. The number doesn't match. He always stores any number he needs. Unlike his lines, he can never remember numbers.

"411, Gaby, how can I help you today?" Another Gaby at information. Were they all given the same name, maybe to make things easier?

"It's Frank, can you please tell me the name that goes with the following number?" He slowly reads the number, as clearly as he can, and hears Gaby typing it in.

"Do you want the name and address sent to your phone as a text message, sir?"

"That would be great, Gaby, and have a nice evening in New York!" He guesses Gaby is going to reply, but he hangs up before she can and waits for the message to get to his Blackberry. Maybe Gaby is upset at him for just hanging up, because the message doesn't come. "Aw, c'mon! Is she nuts?" Frank tosses the phone onto the kitchen counter in annoyance, grabs the bottle of lemon water and goes down the marble steps, shaking his head. Just as he puts his foot on the bottom step, he hears the Blackberry humming from above. "You can kiss my ass, Gaby!" he curses to himself. But his curiosity gets the better of him and he goes back up the steps. He picks up his cell phone, opens the message and frowns in confusion. When he gets back down to the sauna, he lets the towel fall and steps into the hot steam, taking a deep breath of the wonderful smell. He puts his mind to trying to remember if he has ever heard the name Simon Zimmermann before...

CHAPTER 14

I jerk awake, run to the bathroom and throw up the contents of my stomach into the toilet bowl! I can't stop retching, even when nothing more will come. After a good five minutes, that seem like forever to me, I stand, exhausted from throwing up, wash my face with cold water and look at my pale face in the mirror. I don't look good, not good at all. My eyes seem to have tried to escape, and have now returned to my head for some strange reason, making the shadows below them stand out even more. My almond skin seems to have lost its healthy glow. What even was that? The three first months of morning sickness are long over. What did I eat yesterday? I quickly run all the meals of the day through my mind, and notice with horror how much of my appetite I've lost, and how often I forget to eat entirely, from being busy and other things. Apart from my evening meal with Roberto, what did we eat, again? As I'm trying to remember, I weigh myself and smile contentedly, I can't see the gauge because my belly is in the way. I bend forward, less than 135 pounds! That isn't possible, I get off and back on. The same weight appears in the little window. I never weighed less then 139 pounds before becoming pregnant. Just the right weight for my height of 5'4", not skinny, but still a healthy BMI. How could I let this happen. What did I even eat yesterday evening?

"Dr. Dubois is in an operation, and he won't be out for some time. Would you like to try again later, or can I take a message for him?" I ask them to have my doctor call me back, and I hang up. Shit, shit, and once again, shit! This can't be happening!

Today of all days, with the flight booked, Roberto and Simon are making all kinds of plans, my condition has gotten worse. And the fact that I still haven't told my husband everything doesn't help my unease. I'm pacing back and forth in my office when the phone rings.

"Steiner?" I answer, my voice betraying how upset I feel.

"Hey, what's with you?" I hear Roberto's friendly voice ask. "Are you okay? Did I ring at a bad time?" I sit down in the chair and hold the receiver tight to my cheek... 'You never ring at a bad time...' I think, and listen as he softly says, "Jasmin, what's going on, something's wrong, isn't it! Did something happen this morning? I'm sorry I had to go so early, did you see your breakfast, and my note?"

'Yes,' I think. 'It's good you left so early, and yes, I did see the breakfast you so thoughtfully made for me, though I couldn't eat a bite after throwing up.' I quickly try to say something, before my long pause makes him even more worried. "I'm fine, I'm just a bit preoccupied with a problem I have to solve."

"I can help! You educated types always have such interesting problems. Solving them is fun for me, like a detective story. Tell me, let your guru help you!" I sigh, but I can't help smiling, even though the smile almost makes me burst into tears.

"Okay. Imagine two students are studying for a very difficult test. They are both studying together, but each in their own way. The exam is very difficult and they have to try and learn as much of the theory as they can. Okay, one of the students has a meeting with the professor and gets some additional information, but the student doesn't think it is relevant. He doesn't know what he should do. Should he tell his classmate about the information, which will just confuse him and distract him from the relevant facts. Or should he keep the meeting to himself and just study with the other student?" I bite my lower lip, run my free hand through my unruly hair until it is buried in there. The tension on the line is unbearable, and I can hear Roberto's breath on the other end.

"Hm... the other student might be very disappointed, especially if it turns out that the information could have been helpful. On the other hand, what I don't know can't hurt me. So student 'A' could keep it to himself either way, it's a win-win. He passes the test AND has a new study buddy! Of course, it would be bad if the professor brought it up with both students. That would really put a damper on things... so how does my solution sound?" Roberto waits excitedly for my response... but something he said is still going round in my head 'put a damper on things'.

"That's great, you're an ideal student! We'll see what the students think. But I can see the problem is clear and understandable, thanks, you've been a big help! How are things with you? Did everybody make it?"

"Yes, one is really hanging by a thread, his poor wife. They aren't much older than us. We really have to talk about this sort of thing, what you or I should decide, if one of us is being kept alive by machines. There are a few other medical decisions we have to make, as well, before the baby comes, okay? Let's do that tonight? I think it's important, after an operation like that, it really makes you think. Okay, I have to get back, and you, don't confuse your students with the problems you set them!"

"Okay, let's do that! I love you! See you later!"

As expected, Dr. Dubois wants to see me today. We arrange an appointment at six in the evening. That leaves me some time beforehand to arrange all the administrative things I have to do. My thoughts keep wandering, and the conversation Roberto wants to have tonight makes me feel uneasy. My stomach hurts and a stab of pain makes me jump to my feet. 'What now? Please, please, not now.....OHHHH yes, now!! Please, please, again!!' I am so touched, it's the first time my baby has kicked me! I can't keep back the tears of joy, and I throw open the door between me and Claudia, "Claudia, my baby is moving! I felt it, come here!" Two long-fingered hands are on my belly almost the moment I speak.

"Hello little one! Are you giving mommy a hard time? I'm Claudia and I'm so happy you're here!" She strokes my bump and grins at me. "It's a wonderful feeling, isn't it? Oh, oh, I felt something! And again! Whoa, this is a wild one! It has to be a girl, definitely, I've already got money on it." I can't believe how it feels. I always wondered if I would feel it, and if it would be a good feeling, or painful. I can hardly wait for Roberto to feel it! His first contact with his child. I consider blowing off the appointment with Dr. Dubois. I don't want to loose this high tonight, and I wonder what excuse I should make. Tomorrow would be just as good, after all...

CHAPTER 15

"Simon Zimmermann? It's Frank Conley. You tried to ring me yesterday?" Frank is sitting with his morning coffee alongside a freshly squeezed fruit shake, ham, tomatoes, and scrambled eggs. He still makes sure he has a healthy, balanced breakfast, accompanied by exercise and some sauna time. He also likes to go for a run with Freja early in the morning, then the breakfast and off to work with a clear head and a spring in his step. He used to do this every day, even when he had to be on set early in the morning, he went to bed early so he could get up and fit in his run before daybreak. Today things are a little different. He doesn't make so many films anymore, and he's got used to reading the paper in bed and easing comfortably into the day. But he doesn't really have as much energy these days, and he feels it if he does some exercise in the afternoon. Maybe he will have to start getting some discipline back into his mornings.

At the latest, when his next movie is slated to start filming and he finds out how in shape he is going to have to be for the role.

"Mr. Conley, thank you for calling me back. It's an honor, sir!"

'This can not be happening,' Frank thinks! 'Not a stalker, or some other kind of freak! He has a strange accent. Time to change his cell number again! What idiot gave him my number?' "Where did you get this number?" Frank asks, as politely as he can muster.

"From Coney Island Hospital, sir." Frank freezes, suddenly alert.

"Go ahead, Simon," Frank says, tension in his voice.

"I've been an OR assistant at Coney Island Hospital for almost two years, and I'm in the middle of my training. I'm looking for an interesting case for my dissertation, and I heard about the accident yesterday. Who hasn't!" Frank realizes he still hasn't seen the news, but it seems everyone is talking about what happened.

"Go on," he tells the man on the other end of the phone.

"I work in a different department," the man continues, "which means I don't have access to the ICU, and so I can't see the patients. I'm not allowed to talk to them. I can look at the notes, with permission, of course, but the patients are off limits."

Frank can't work out the reason for the call, certainly not one that would involve him, and he tells the man so, "What has this got to do with me?"

"I read that you found the victim, and visited her in the hospital." Was that the sort of thing people made a note of in the patient's notes? Frank is a little shocked. "Your name and telephone number were in there, too, in case there was no contact from relatives." Now Frank is completely bewildered. Contact person, in case there is no word from the family? Why? What did he have to do with the victim, all he had done was find her. He starts to feel uneasy, even though he has to admit he feels a connection with the victim. Especially after what Susie had told him.

"Okay, so what do you want from me, Simon? You're obviously calling me in a private capacity."

"Yes, exactly, that's right, I'm not allowed to have any personal contact with the victim, and that's what I need. I need information from the patient for my dissertation, so I wanted to ask you if you would be able to provide me with that information. This is a serious, professional work of medical science, so all I'm interested in are the facts of her case. Of course, I would provide you with all my material before it is published, and nobody's real name will be used. Everything will be anonymous."

"Why would I be allowed to talk to the patient?" Frank really doesn't see what this man is getting at. "Her family will be speaking to her. Why don't you ask them?" Frank finishes off his fruit shake while he listens to Simon clearing his throat, and he gets the feeling the man is gulping hard, his throat dry. He sounds nervous. Because of Frank?

"There is no family, Mr. Conley, at least not yet." Now it's Frank's turn to gulp.

"Nobody has made contact yet? Has she even been reported missing? Twenty-four hours are already up, since yesterday evening."

"Yes I know, that's why I'm contacting you," Simon says, trying again to explain. Frank rests his head in his free hand and looks out at the garden and the ocean. What in hell is going on here? His thoughts are building up like the waves outside, impossible to get a clear picture of. "Are you still there?" Simon's funny accent is insistent in his ear.

"Yes, I'm still here. This all sounds strange to me, I can't help you right now, Simon, I'm sorry. I have to get my head round all this myself first, and I have to contact the police."

"Okay, that's fine. I understand," Simon replies, obviously disappointed. "But could I please ask you not to tell anyone about my request? If anyone found out about this, I would lose my job." Frank's eyebrows go up in surprise.

"The same goes for you, kid. Delete my number! If I feel I can help you, I'll ring you, okay?" It all sounds like something from one of my movies, Frank thinks with a contented smile. "One more thing, where are you from? I've never heard an accent like yours before."

"Sure, I'll delete it, you have my word. I'm from Switzerland."

Frank can not reach Officer Tropman, so he tries calling Susie. He gets a machine. She must already be at the hospital, so he looks up the number for Coney Island Hospital, stores it in his phone, and then rings it. "Coney Island Hospital, this is Susan. How can I help you?" Susie's voice sounds so professional and helpful. Frank is already gleefully anticipating her reaction when she finally recognizes his voice as he disguises it.

"Susan, today is your lucky day! You have won a flight over New York!" He hears her giggling, but he keeps his composure.

"You don't say! When do we set off, my superhero?" she says the last part quietly, and Frank realizes she has already worked out it's him.

"Whenever you have time for me! How are you today, Susie? Did you have a good breakfast?" Frank takes a sip of his third espresso of the morning and takes the cup into the bedroom with him.

"If Mr. Perfect thinks two donuts and a half a liter of Walmart coffee is a good breakfast, then yes! How about you? Have you finished your beauty routine? I wouldn't mind being a fly on the wall when a film star drags his famous butt out of bed. Hang on, There's a call on the other line." Frank hears a click and classical music starts playing.

He wonders if there is much difference between their morning routines. He wonders about her idea of his morning routine. After visiting her home, he is sure she would be a little overwhelmed if she visited his home. Most people are, when they see it for the first time, and Frank always thinks it is way too big for him alone. A family should live here, with children to fill the place with laughter and music. Parents, who liked to entertain, and who could one day invite all their grandchildren to have fun in the pool, play on the tennis court, and enjoy the breathtaking view from every room. That was how he imagined it would be when Ken was still young. Then came the accident, and there was no wife, or any more children to make this dream come true. "Still there, daydreamer?" Susie's voice interrupts Frank's thoughts, and the hold music.

"What do you mean, daydreamer? When do you have time?"

"What would I be making time for?" Susie whispers, after a few seconds' pause.

"Well, for the flight over New York, of course. I wasn't joking. I'd like you to see the city from the air, if you want?" Frank feels like an idiot again for being so sure that the fun and exciting Susie would want to take a flight with him, just like that. He hopes he hasn't offended her again by suggesting it.

"Holy shit, Frankie, what's going on here? Am I Pretty Woman now, except not so young, or so pretty, which makes you Richard Gere, except even better? Or did you just feel sorry for me yesterday, and now you want to show an ordinary, every-day woman how rich people live?" He has offended her, he feels terrible about how he's messed up again.

"No, Susie, nothing like that. I just wanted to find a way to make a connection. I really like you! Nothing more, nothing less. I really enjoy flying, and I thought it would be nice to have some company on a flight over the city. Because you're fun to be around! You're a real breath of fresh air to me! But we can easily forget it, I don't want to make you uncomfortable. I can take no for an answer." Susie laughs out loud, as if she wants to share this with the whole of reception.

"I can take no for an answer!" she imitates him. "Frank you're such a smooth talker, I could just eat you up when you're being serious like this! I'll hop in a plane in a second with you, prince charming, and fly over the city! Hey, but don't cry if I vomit the whole time, all over the plane. Mama don't like to fly, you know! But, if you have the time, why don't we fly to the South Seas for a week, or just for a cocktail at sunset!" She laughs again, and Frank thinks he'd better not mention that he really could arrange for them to fly to the South Seas and that the sunsets there are breathtaking.

CHAPTER 16

I climb the stairs to our apartment on the fourth floor with bouncing strides, hardly able to wait to feel our baby move with Roberto, then I hear loud music and movement inside our home. What is he doing, making so much noise? I open the front door and the music hits me in the face like a wall. I hear Roberto training on the weight bench in his gym. What is going on with my husband, I think, as I take off my shoes and coat then go towards all the sweaty activity. The closer I get, the louder and more unnerving the situation seems, and I start to have a bad feeling in my belly. I see Roberto, bathed in sweat, lying on the weight bench, repeatedly pushing weights of at least 220 pounds into the air and letting them fall again. Something must have happened, I've never seen him like this. I go over to the stereo, to turn down the music, and Roberto screams at me, "Don't even think about it! I'm not done yet!" What the...? Did he just scream at me? Shocked and upset, I hurry out of the room and go to the kitchen. What was that about? I have never seen or heard my husband like that. In all our seven years, he has never raised his voice to me, or shown me such a lack of respect. I get a glass of water and drink it in slow sips, while I try to ignore the loud music and sounds of exercise. I put my glass in the dishwasher and I am about to leave the kitchen when I see an open envelope on the counter. There is sheet of paper, unfolded, with sections marked in ballpoint. My brow wrinkles in confusion and I slowly go over to the sheet of paper. I get close enough to read the envelope and all the blood runs from my face, my knees go weak, and I can hear my heart beat faster, even over the loud music. I pick up the folded piece of paper with shaking hands and try to force my teary eyes to focus. It is the test results from the lab. And Roberto has read them. My vision fades and I notice the music stopping abruptly. Roberto is now standing in front of me, bathed in sweat, he quickly wipes his face and hair with a towel, and his big blue eyes pierce my beating heart.

"When, Jasmin, when? When were you going to tell me?" His voice, usually so loving, deep, and reassuring now sounds penetrating, harsh, and threatening.

"I, I..." my voice is about to give out, I have to force it not to desert me, "I just couldn't, Roberto. I was already pregnant when I found out. I just didn't want to believe it, I still don't. There is...."

Roberto hurls the towel to the floor in anger and comes at me, "You didn't want to believe it? You've known for more than four months. What is this, are you nuts? We had an excellent chance, and you didn't want to believe it? I can't believe what I'm hearing!" He runs his hands through his hair and tears come to his still furious eyes. "Do you know what you are doing to us, to ME? I'm an OR assistant, I understand this stuff!" he picks up the piece of paper and throws it at my feet! "Who do you think you are, playing god like this? I always thought I had a wife with a brain in her head, and I was glad. But this! Jasmin, I can hardly look at you!" He suddenly turns and disappears into the bathroom, and I hear the shower three seconds later.

I'm still standing, frozen, in the kitchen when Roberto comes back, dry, in a t-shirt and jeans. He goes past me, picks up my glass and fills it with water. He empties it in one gulp. Then he leaves the kitchen again, pauses for a moment with his back to me, and his voice is a little calmer. "Okay, if you don't have anything else to say, then I'll go. I won't be back today, I'm just going to forget about tonight, I can't stand the dishonest atmosphere in this apartment right now!"

"Roberto, please! Of course I have something to say, I have a lot to say! Do you remember the exercise with the two students, studying for a test?" Roberto frowns, until he suddenly remembers and he looks at me, eyes wide in shock.

"You were talking about us? Dammit, Jasmin, how sneaky are you? I don't know you anymore! You use such an underhanded trick to get me to say 'okay' to your secrets and lies? And then you dare to compare our child to some school test? I'm completely at a loss..."

"No, listen to me! Right from the start I was convinced everything would be okay! I'm already in the fifth month, and everything is going fine! I'm doing fine! And hey, I felt the first kick, and I could hardly wait for you to feel for yourself this evening! We're doing fine! Really!" I watch in horror as Roberto balls his hand into a fist, and it looks for a moment as though he is going to raise it.

"You're so naive, so incredibly naive and brutal! I can't imagine what Dr. Dubois thinks about me, supporting you in this craziness!"

"He knows I haven't told you, not yet, and he absolutely doesn't agree with me. So it's not just you who thinks I'm a complete idiot, if that puts your mind at rest!"

"At rest? Damn, Jasmin!" Roberto's jugular is worryingly engorged and he bends his head in my direction, coming down to my eye line to make sure I understand what he is about to yell at me, and that I'm taking him seriously. "You have breast cancer! And this evil thing is growing with every day of your pregnancy! Neither of you are going to survive unless we do something, if there is even anything that can be done! Breast cancer! Do you understand! And if it has metastasized, that means it's spread everywhere! What were you thinking?"

"There are five percent who do okay! I'm one of the five percent! That's what I thought..." As I am speaking, I feel a wave of painful realization! I feel pain at the suffering my body has brought to Roberto's present, and his future. The lost hope that I have been so desperately clinging to, and the positive energy that has accompanied me over the preceding months. It's all falling apart, like a house of cards, and being washed away in the stream behind our building.

I sob from the pain, cry, and wish for nothing more than to find comfort in Roberto's arms. Those strong arms, that are so close and yet so far. Roberto goes into the bathroom and splashes some cold water on his face. He has been crying as well, and he swallows the rest of his tears. He goes into the bedroom and comes back into the living room wearing a pullover. "I need some time to think, so get something to eat, and get to bed early! Try to keep your strength up, as long as you can. I'm going out for a while." He looks at me, sadness in his eyes and his look almost rips my heart in two.

"Roberto please, stay with us. Let's talk about it, let me explain, don't just leave us." He puts on his shoes and a coat. "Roberto, please say something! We can make more plans for New York, let's not be pessimistic now!"

He shoots me a glance, the last of the night, and says, softly but clearly, "There will be no New York for you. You are staying here, near Dr. Dubois! I need some time to think, you have a four month head start on me!"

CHAPTER 17

"That was by far the best lunch break I have ever had in my life! Honey, you are a sweetheart, I could just hug you!" Susie's smile spreads across her face as they return to the Maybach from the helicopter pad! She holds her big handbag as elegantly as possible and tries to make a good impression. Frank has often wondered what women have in their big handbags. They always look full and he can't imagine what could be inside, apart from a cell phone, money, and ID. Some makeup, maybe, lipstick and stuff like that? He could ask Susie, she would give him an honest answer.

"You liked it? Beautiful! Doesn't the city just look amazing from above?"

"Whoa, you sappy dope, you're telling me? And not just the city! Did you see the houses outside? Some of them had their own golf course or tennis court!" Frank bites his lower lip and once again thinks about how refreshing and down to earth she is! The driver holds open the back door of the car for her and, of course, she can't help but say something. "Hey, you in the uniform, I'm getting in the back and I don't want to be disturbed with the boss, okay?"

Lou winks at her, "Understood," he says.

Susie gabs about all kinds of things on the way to the hospital. After quickly stopping to draw breath, she gives Frank a penetrating look and asks, "Have you heard about what's been going on at the hospital? Nobody has contacted us abut your victim. She's lying in the ICU, and nobody even misses her! I mean, what kind of family must she come from? If my boys left me to rot like that, with a bunch of strangers, there would be hell to pay!" Frank tries to look surprised, so as not to give away Simon's call.

"What do you think, should I try again at the intensive care unit? Do you think, in these circumstances, would they allow me to see her?" Frank stares at the woman in the car with him, his gaze searching, wondering at the same time whether he even wants that.

"Yes, do that! She's so alone up there, poor kid! Hey, and after all, you are the man who saved her life and the last one to see her alive! I mean alive, to speak to...or something like that. Ah, what do I know, I can't even let myself imagine it, Frankie, what you must have seen! If I think about it, I'll just get sick and mess up your nice limo...but honestly, I know you can't answer such a horrible question, but what kind of sicko does something like that?" Susie's agitation and worry was starting to give Frank a headache. He takes her hand and holds it reassuringly.

"I don't know, Susie, but you're right, I should try and visit her. And who knows, maybe somebody will come and be with her there when she wakes up. Maybe they're on holiday, or there is some other reason they can't visit her, or maybe there was a fight, and she's not in contact with them right now..." While he is trying to come up with things that could make Susie feel better, he thinks about the longest time he went without hearing from Ken.

"Lou, I'll go in as well. It could be a while. If I'm not going to be back in 15 minutes, I'll let you know." The driver nods to Frank and opens the door for Susie in front of the Coney Island Hospital.

"See you Lou," she yells, "it was fun! Stay safe, the streets of New York are dangerous! I don't want to see your name on a set of patient's notes." Lou nods, smiling, and gently closes the door again. Before he can go round to the other side, Frank has already gotten out and closed the door to keep up with Susie. They go through the main entrance together, the first time he has seen it during the day. Susie's desk looks as friendly and inviting as her. The person covering for Susie gets up as she comes in the door, almost as if she shouldn't be sitting in her chair. Susie settles in to her station, beams at Frank through her glasses and says, "I won't tell anyone about our romantic date, or what happened on the back seat, honey! Should I ring Leslie?" Before Frank can thank her for accompanying him on the flight, she picks up the phone and hits speed dial for an internal number. Her movements are so natural and habitual, and Frank wonders if he has any habitual movements ingrained in him from his job.

"What's going on hon? Yes, I went out for lunch." Susie gives Frank a mischievous wink, "I'll tell you another time. Every woman needs her secrets, you have them too!

Apart from right now, tell me, what is happening with our Jane Doe? Has anyone contacted you? Has she woken up? ... oh... holy shit... so horrible?... how long? ... hm... hey, you think, under these circumstances, the man who found her could sit with her a while. I mean, the poor child, so alone...and they would hear, right?... Yes, I understand.... yes, he is...I know, but you know me! Leslie, if it was one of my kids, I wouldn't want it just to be white coats round him, they're in this horror show because it's their job! There has to be someone human there... yes, I know you are, but you have to understand...okay, that's what I wanted to hear! That's my Leslie! Thanks!" She puts down the phone, blinks at the screen and types something. "She'll talk to the doctor on duty. And I can see that's Dr. Shilling today. Perfect, a cute Irish guy, he'll be kind enough to allow you in, he's got his heart in the right place. And I think Leslie reminds him of his mom, back in Ireland. He can never say no to her.... or maybe the old girl just makes him nervous!" Susie shrugs and giggles. She looks happy. She really did enjoy the trip. Frank is glad such a simple gesture can make somebody so happy. He gives her a thumbs up and looks at his blinking Blackberry. A message from Tom, new scripts to read, suggested appointments for meetings, a missed call from

Ken, who has left a voice massage asking how he is, and a missed call from Officer Tropman.

"Susie, just imagine..." the telephone behind the counter rings, an internal call that Susie answers. She listens for a while then hangs up. She stands up and lets her glasses fall on their chain. She puts her hand on Frank's.

"You'd better get yourself a big cup of coffee from the cafeteria, superhero! You have now been officially allowed access to INT7! It's going to be a long afternoon, I hope you're good at telling stories!" She pats his hand and blows him a kiss. "Hasta la vista, baby! I know, it's not from one of your films, but it fits!"

Chapter 18

Unsettled, sad and feeling miserable, I wander round the whole house. He can't be serious! I have to stay here while he and Simon have fun in New York, without me? He can't do that! That was...IS our trip! Our last trip as a couple without a child. And how dare he doubt my strength? He sees everything so negative, he isn't giving a positive attitude a chance. My sadness has quickly turned into anger and I stride into my home office and sit at my laptop. Direct flights to New York appear on the screen, and I scroll through the options. 'Okay, if I have to travel alone, I might as well do it in style. I refuse to be left at home!' I type in my dates, select business class and then look at hotels. I click through several options and decide on the Marriott in Times Square. 'Okay, how about a musical? The Phantom of the Opera would be amazing, so I book a ticket. Oh, what's this? A helicopter trip above New York? Just 100 dollars? Well, it only lasts ten minutes, but who cares?' I book that as well. I complete the purchase and pay with a credit card. 'That's how it's done! You don't just shut me out!'

Making the booking feels good, at first, but just a few minutes later I am overcome by guilt and I'm angry with myself for being so childish. Roberto has good reason to be angry. How would she have reacted if he had kept a secret like this from her? Am I really so naive? Did I really delude myself so badly? I've never been a devil may care type. How could I have felt so good about the whole thing when everybody else has a completely different opinion. I have to speak with somebody, someone I can trust, not somebody with medical training or somebody who works in medicine...a mother, a woman who understands what this is really about...and just then I'm being kicked from the inside. A gentle nudge in the side, then a gentle nudge in the other side. How beautiful it feels. "Hello, who's is this then? This is your mom. What's that, your head or your leg? What do you think, who should I call?" I gently and lovingly stroke my hands over my belly, touching my baby where it is moving. It's a shame that Roberto can't be here to experience this, he would have loved it. Instead, he's in some bar having a beer or two, asking himself what he has done wrong to deserve... me? Another kick, more powerful than before, and I see Claudia appear before my eyes. Yes, Claudia will understand! She has four kids, still works and she's very sympathetic. A glance at my slim watch tells me it isn't too late to call her.

"Van Thiel?" Claudia's son, one of the three, picks up.

"It's Jasmin, which of you boys is this?"

"Marc, hello Jasmin. Is everything okay?"

"Yes, thanks! How are things at school? You'll be graduating soon, right?"

"No, that's Fin, I'm training to work in a chemical laboratory. Do you want to talk to my mom? She's not here. She's at Yoga, or Zumba or the book club or something. Do you want me to find out where?"

"Yes, thanks Marc."

I hear him go a few steps and flick through pages, probably the family wall planner. An impressive woman! How does she do it? Four great kids, work and still time for her hobbies. I don't have a child yet and I find it difficult to make time for my hobbies. Does going out for a nice meal count as a hobby? If not, then I'm really in trouble. I don't have time to practice piano anymore, so all I can play is what I've already learned...I used to like fixing up old things. I should take that up again. I should get something from a thrift shop and make it nice for our apartment. I can decorate the baby's room. I feel a wave of anticipation when I hear Marc's voice again.

"Okay, today is definitely yoga. She'll be finished at 9:15, and the gym is nearby. She'll be home by 9:30 p.m., she showers here. Should I get her to call you when she gets here?" I think for a moment and say no. We both say goodnight and hang up.

It's a good time to go for an evening walk, to get some fresh air and go find Claudia. I've never had a best friend, I suddenly think, as I am putting on my coat and shoes. And the coat soon won't fit. I struggle to get the buttons fastened over my belly and wrap a big scarf round my neck, and let it drape down over the straining buttons, but it still isn't a particularly elegant picture. Various different schools, exchange programs abroad, then university and moving to a new town have all played a part in me not having a best friend. I have always had lots of people and friends in my life, but never a best friend who has shared my life since childhood. I have never been a part of a clique of girls either or went out with the girls at night. I always like it when there are lots of different kinds of people, it keeps the conversation interesting. I take a deep breath of the fresh air, and I realize I have forgotten to eat anything again. I take the tram and go a few stops until I see the gym. There is a bar and a place to sit right next to the entrance. I get a fruit shake and some muesli. There isn't much else available. I wonder where Roberto is and what he is having for dinner. The thought causes me a stab of pain and I hope I can make up with him soon. I sit in a chair with a good view of the door that Claudia will soon be coming out of.

CHAPTER 19

Following Susie's advice, Frank finds his way through the hospital to the Cafeteria. When he finally sees the glass door where, judging by the clothes, a lot of the staff are having coffee break, he hesitates to go in. Should he really go to the ICU and sit by the victim? What was he going to say to her? Should he tell her about his house, about Freja, that it was him who found her? Should he read her a book or just be silent? What about physical contact? Can he hold the hand of a perfect stranger? He doesn't think he can. He turns on his heel and calls Lou, as he pushes the button for the elevator.

"Mr. Conley, stop there!" He didn't want to have to creep past Susie's desk, and it seems convenient to him that she is on the phone. "What's going on?" Susie gives him a stern look from behind her glasses. Frank slowly goes over to her and leans against the counter.

"What's going on?" he grins at her. "Are you watching me?" She lets the glasses fall and looks at the main entrance, then back at Frank.

"Were you planning to just creep away? Just like that. You didn't go to the ICU, Leslie rang me, and here you are, coming back without even being gone long enough to glance through the window. Okay, superhero, I'm listening?"

"Well, you see, I wanted to go see her, but I started to get really frightened I'd be stopped by security, by Manders, and look, I just got caught. She's going to rip me a new one!" She doesn't look happy with Frank's answer, and she gives him the side eye, eyebrow arched. "Don't worry Susie, Lou will be here any minute. But he's not here to pick me up. I asked him to get a beautiful bunch of flowers and a big teddy bear. I can't go up empty handed on such an important visit! At my age, I wouldn't dare go to a sick woman's bedside without flowers, otherwise there's no chance of a friendship. Did I pass the test?" For a second Frank has the feeling he can see tears welling up in Susie's eyes. She gives him a trusting pat on the hand, sits on her chair and puts her glasses on her nose.

"A real gentleman!" she murmurs, "Get going, get out of here! Before I start crying!"

With a big bunch of colorful flowers and a teddy bear with the word Ted stitched on it, Frank gets into the elevator for the fourth floor. He feels a tingle go through his body, he's excited. But why? He has no idea how this is going to go, or how he is going to react. He wonders if she is awake. He wonders if her condition has improved or if it has gotten worse? *Ding* The door slides open to reveal the sterile, deathly silent ICU. The staff again seem to be walking on clouds, everything happening with incredible calm, and at a leisurely pace. Frank slowly walks down the corridor in the direction of INT7, following the route he still remembers. Leslie comes to meet him and smiles at him.

"Mr Conley, it's nice to see you again. I'm pleased we could fix it for you to keep the poor woman company for a while. It's so sad that nobody has been in contact. It's been two days already. I'll tell Dr. Shilling that you're here, and he'll come to see you. But go on in, it's okay. I'll take the flowers and find a vase for them. I'm sorry but they can't go in the room, not in the ICU. I'll put them over here, on the counter, so she can see them from the room, okay?" Frank nods, gives her the flowers and slowly walks toward the room containing the unknown victim.

Frank puts Ted on a small table in the corner and grabs the chair beside it, which he brings over and puts beside the bed with the motionless human form in it. She is tucked up in a blanket, right up to the shoulders, with a little bit of her nightgown poking out and a delicate neck, covered in bruises. He can't make out her face, there is a bandage wrapped round her entire head, with tubes coming from the hidden nose and the half-open mouth. From close up, Frank is no longer surprised he couldn't tell from the distance if it was a woman or a man. The heart monitor is rhythmically blinking beside the bed and there is a kind of bellow that inflates and deflates behind it. There's another device with a monitor that Frank doesn't recognize, displaying lines that look like waves. The steady pumping of the bellow combined with the beeping of the monitors gives the room an aura of threat. Frank slowly shakes his head while he gazes at the woman, from head to toe.

"What the hell have you been through? Who did this to you, and why? I'm so sorry, so, so sorry! If there's anything I can do for you, I'll be only too happy to do it. Nobody deserves to end up like this! In fact, not even an animal deserves this. I'm so sorry!" Frank has to fight back the tears. Now, sitting beside her, the things he said to Susie in her comfortable living room seem so strange, like a bad movie, a movie he would never accept a role in, especially now that he is with a real person, a woman, so close to death, watching her chest rising and falling.

Frank gazes at the form for a long time, trying to form an image of the woman, trying to work out what she must look like. He sees from her hands that she must be quite slim, which is confirmed by how little of the bed she takes up. She isn't very tall, and her skin tone is too light to be African American, and it doesn't look like she is Latina, perhaps she is mixed race. Her nails look well cared for, regularly manicured and undamaged by manual labor. With her tucked up in bed, there isn't much more for him to see, and he is surprised at himself for how interested his gaze is. He tries to remember her whimpering on the beach, he lays his hand on her body and again sadly shakes his head. The door to the room silently opens and a tall man of around 50 comes in, dressed in a white coat. He stands at the end of the bed and holds out his hand toward Frank.

"No need to get up, I'm Dr. Shilling, I'm head of medicine here. I'm glad you managed to make time to come here. They tell me you found her on the beach and brought her here?" Frank sits back down in his chair and nods, while he turns his head to look at her again. "I can't tell you all the details, I'm afraid, because we are still hoping to hear from her family. But I can tell you she lost a lot of blood and must have been through a lot of pain. This horrific act of savagery that you stumbled across has been a very challenging case, and she isn't out of the woods yet. She will have to undergo several further operations, and we hope her condition is going to remain stable long enough for that to be possible. First, we had to put her into a medically induced coma, to keep her alive. She just wouldn't have been strong enough to make it otherwise. I'm sure she can hear everything we say, even if she might not be exactly able to remember it later. So go ahead and talk to her about her rescue, or read her some nice stories. Sing to her, if you want, and hold her hand. Human contact is incredibly important for recovery. If you need anything, or if you have any other questions, just press here." He indicates a red button that is hanging above the bed.

Frank suddenly gets up from the chair and looks round the grim little room, then asks, "How long will she be in a medically induced coma?"

CHAPTER 20

Things are tense between Roberto and me, which hasn't often happened before in our relationship. Our situation is unusual, of course, and I'm heartened by the fact that he speaks politely to me, even if he doesn't speak often. He's just as interested as ever in my health, he is happy about the ever stronger movements of our baby, and he is still excited when we visit Dr. Dubois for 'baby watching'. Of course I realize that all he is interested in is our unborn child, but I am an essential part of making sure the child is healthy and he accepts that. Time heals all wounds, his, ours, and mine. And who knows what the future will bring? Talking to Claudia has also made me feel better, reassured me that I'm doing the right thing, but also made me realize that I have to dedicate myself to my family. Roberto and I have done a lot of talking about the next steps we're going to take, and discussed my results. The trip to New York has been a bone of contention, and he refused to change his mind, so we canceled the booking I made, along with the travel insurance. Dr. Kunz has asked me to come see him in his office this afternoon.

"Now it's time to talk turkey!" Claudia said, giving me a quizzical look, as though she could tell I was worried.

"You aren't really wondering if you're going to get the job or not, are you? You know, I don't want to be nosy, and don't take this the wrong way, but it's just a question of probabilities! Even my youngest girl, Alette can manage that calculation! There is a job, and there is a candidate who can do it. What is the likelihood that this candidate will get the job? Why are you still thinking about that? This is just a formality, about politics and stuff, that's just so the big cheeses on the board of directors can also have a say. You know what I'm talking about! Why do you think they get the big bucks?" She shakes her head in exasperation, rolls her eyes and turns her attention back to her computer. She's right of course, there isn't a lot of competition for the job. I've been here the longest and I have the most experience in a management role. Again, Claudia has made me feel a lot better, and I go back to my office, where a ringing telephone is waiting for me.

"Steiner!"

"Hello, Mrs. Steiner, it's de Almeida, your online travel consultant. I'm not sure if there has been some kind of mix-up, but we have two different bookings in your name for a return trip to New York on two different dates. One was canceled, but the one for the later date is still on the system, and the credit card payment has already been processed. Has there been some kind of mistake?" My god, they look at every little detail! It's a good thing I gave them my phone as a contact number. I wouldn't be allowed back in the house if it came out I had been keeping more secrets.

"No, that's right, it's fine! I just had to push back the date, but thanks for keeping such a close eye on things"

"But your traveling companion, Mr. Garreffa, is he keeping the original booking?"

"That's right, he's flying out before me," I say, with a guilty conscience and wait for them to hang up, but the Nancy Drew of Swiss Airlines has more questions to ask.

"You also booked a room at the Marriott Hotel for the duration of the entire trip, but there is no room for Mr. Garretta for the two days he will be there before you arrive. Is that what you want, or would you like to extend the reservation two days earlier in his name?" It would be great if every call center operator took their job this seriously. I imagine she is a trainee who is still so keen to work for an online travel agent that she is making the impossible possible!

"No, that's okay, he'll be staying with a friend for those two days. This is all very observant of you Ms. Meida!"

"De Almeida," she says, and I can just imagine how happy they are with her at the call center. I get a bottle of Rimus and some delicious canapes, then I go up the stairs to our loft, more slowly now than before. Roberto is home before me again, and I imagine how great it would be if I and the child could wait for father to come home. I open the door and I can hear Roberto speaking. I can't make out what he's saying, and I don't know who he's talking to, but it sounds like a professional conversation from the tone of his voice. It is taking me longer and longer to struggle out of my coat and shoes, and to put them away.

As I get closer, he says goodbye to whoever is on the other end of the line with the words, "Thank you very much, and goodbye Mrs.... sorry, your name has slipped my mind for a moment, yes, that's right, sorry." He hangs up.

"Hi, who was that?" I ask, as I go to give him a kiss, that he skillfully avoids.

"Hello, I have a cold coming on, you shouldn't get to close." He gently strokes my belly and says, "The online travel agent is offering me an upgrade to business class because I have so many miles." He looks at me with his big blue eyes, as if he is expecting some kind of reaction, and I don't disappoint him.

"That's great! Wow, you can lie down and get some sleep, the food will be better, and you'll be fresh when you arrive at Simon's place! Good for you!" I don't want my slightly overenthusiastic euphoria to be suspicious, so I hold up the Rimus and say triumphantly, "And there is something else to celebrate today! Alea iacta est! Which means, the die is cast! The board has decided on the new school head!" I glance sideways at my husband, waiting expectantly.

He doesn't react, he just calmly says, "I'm happy for you! And guess what, I did learn at least some Latin at school! You shouldn't just assume I'm completely ignorant." He takes the bottle from me and goes into the kitchen, where he gets two champagne glasses out of the cupboard.

Chapter 21

"Do you want a game with your old man?" Frank is always happy to hear his son's voice, and he would be even more pleased to see him. They haven't seen each other for a week. Of course, hardly a day has gone by when they haven't talked on the phone or exchanged an email, but the visits to the hospital, two interviews at two different ends of the country, as well as a short trip to Canada with police permission, also for a talk show, have meant this week has gone by in a blur.

"I'd be delighted, if you have time for me?" Frank is hurt by the words, ever if it isn't the first time he's heard them. He doesn't dispute that it's usually his fault if they don't see each other for a while. They agree that Ken will come home and they'll meet at the house's tennis court, and Frank arranges for a pick up by Lou. It usually ruffles Ken's feathers when Frank makes use of his luxurious way of getting round town, but surprisingly today he doesn't say a word.

"I've got so much on my plate right now. I would be happy to be able to use the two hour drive for something useful. Thanks Dad. I'm looking forward to putting you through your paces, and giving you some exercise for your old ticker." His grin makes Frank even happier! People without kids are really missing out, he thinks, and he sighs. He winds up thinking about Linda. Linda, whose life is still hanging by a thread, and all he can do is simply be there for her, whenever he can. He knows that a lot of Ken's work is because of her. His son listens to everything he has to say attentively, and he is so interested, and asks so many questions, that his father realizes that he sees the case as his own. No relatives have yet been in contact, which can't be very comforting to Kenneth.

Frank will go to the city with Ken early that evening to visit Linda. He hopes that he will be able to speak to Dr. Shilling, to get more information about the next stages of treatment. For the moment he decides to keep to himself that, thanks to Susie, he knows a lot more details than the doctor would be allowed to tell him. He has also found out all he can about the artificially induced coma. "The anesthesia is usually continued for several days. After a severe brain injury, however, it can take longer. Usually the swelling on the brain reduces after a matter of weeks," Dr. Shilling tells him. "We will then be able to determine the extent of the damage the patient has suffered." Most of the organs keep functioning during the coma. The heart keeps beating, the liver and the kidneys continue to function. Linda has to be fed through a tube, and has to be helped to breathe. The risk of complications increases as time goes on. The ventilator could cause inflammation of the lungs, and so much time in bed can cause thrombosis. They will try to keep the time the patient is under anesthetic to a minimum, but they can not bring her out of it too early.

Dr. Shilling has always taken so much time to answer all of Frank's questions, which had left Frank feeling that he owed him something. Until Susie brutally set him straight, "You see, honey, not everyone makes as much money as you for a few scenes, but THESE are the scenes Dr. Irish Coffee is interested in! He is well paid for top quality translation of medical jargon into language mere mortals can understand. And that includes you! So no gifts, or you'll just spoil him, and he won't be such a nice doctor anymore!" He has taken what she said to him to heart, and now he makes sure he asks all the questions he wants of Dr. Shilling.

His ticker, as Ken calls his heart, is being put under stress and he is thankful that the young, healthy lawyer is going easy on him. Bathed in sweat with his knees threatening to give way beneath him, he goes the few steps to the bench alongside the tennis court. He slumps onto it and reaches for a bottle of water. "Goddamn kid, that's what I call a beating. I can't let that go unanswered. I want a rematch, as soon as I'm a little more in shape!" Ken wipes his face and his sweaty hair with a towel and laughs.

"You weren't so bad, dad. I had to work for it, you didn't make it easy on me! I'll be happy if I'm as fit as you at your age." He knows he's said something a little fresh and he holds his wet towel up to protect his face.

"Oh, you are going to pay for that, I promise you!" They silently enjoy the feeling of their pounding hearts, the adrenaline in their blood and the cool Atlantic breeze. "Are you coming with me to see Linda today?" Frank blinks at Ken.

"Is that what you are calling her? It' a nice name, Dad, I like it! Why that name?"

"If you come with me, I'll tell you why I call her Linda. It would really mean a lot to me if you would be there with me today. It's never fun to visit her, but I wouldn't miss it. It will be nicer if you come. Do you understand what your old man is trying to say?"

"You don't need to say another word, I'll be happy to go with you. I've heard quite a lot about Linda, and I'd like to meet her in person."

Frank slaps his son on the shoulder. "Now I wouldn't mind something to eat! What do you say to spare ribs, roast potatoes and sour cream, with a couple of cold Budweisers?"

The food gives the two Conley's new energy and they relax in the back of the Maybach as they are driven to Coney Island. "So, Dad, now it's your turn, why are you calling the unknown victim Linda? Have you discovered something? Did Susie find something out, or did you finally ring Officer Tropman back?" Ken quizzes his father expectantly!

CHAPTER 22

"Hey Jasmin, nice to hear from you again! Ready to go?" Simon's voice sounds happy and motivated. But his question is confusing.

"Hello Simon, it's nice to hear you too. What should I be ready for? My due date isn't for two months." I follow this with a little forced laugh, a little uncomfortable with the conversation.

"For New York, of course! Don't act so cool, people don't come to visit me here every day of the week!" It sounds like he is really looking forward to my visit, and I'm getting more confused and uncomfortable with every passing moment.

"Simon, I'm not coming. Didn't Roberto tell you?" I feel a creeping sensation in my stomach and I look in the direction of the kitchen, where Roberto has stopped loading the dishwasher. Has he kept Simon in the dark on purpose? It's not the sort of detail you simply forget, if you have told your wife she can't come on holiday with you, especially considering the reason. Roberto comes over to me, looking concerned and gently shaking his head.

Simon is silent a while, then says, "I don't understand. What did you say, that you aren't coming?" the sound of his excited anticipation disappearing from his voice.

"Hang on, I'll hand you over to Roberto, he's right here. It was nice talking to you, Simon. Take care! Bye!" I hear him say a hesitant goodbye as I sadly pass the receiver to Roberto. I simply turn my back on this little scene and go into the bathroom, crying silently. A hot bath will do me a lot of good. I start filling the tub, throw in a bath pearl, and slowly undress. I can hear the murmur of Roberto's voice and I'm relieved I can't make out the words. Why did he keep this a secret? Or does he know that I'm going to New York as well? It's time we spend a while apart, we aren't as connected as we once were, and there isn't the deep attraction that there once was. But it's true that time heals all wounds, and this crisis will just strengthen our marriage and bring us closer together. As will our shared responsibility for our first child, that we had so desperately longed for.

The evening turns out to be very harmonious. Roberto comes to see us in the bath tub, which we two are filling to the brim, so we hardly need to add much water at all. He tells me why he kept it secret from Simon that I would be staying in Switzerland. There is a reason for everything, his fears, hopes and doubts, which is very illuminating for me. I come close, a couple of times, to telling him that I am going to travel anyway, but I decided against it, so as not to spoil our evening together. We watch an action movie together, nibble on nuts and dried figs, and drink nonalcoholic beer. He gives me a gentle foot massage, which makes me feel even better, and I think to myself that Frank Conley is a gifted and charismatic actor.

I enjoy my lunch break with Claudia on the roof terrace of our school, and we chat about the film we have both seen the night before. "I don't really like action movies, but Conley is just hot, so I'll sit with my boys and watch it. They know why I'm watching, but their mom doesn't have much else to enjoy!" Claudia's joyful attitude is always welcome and I enjoy spending time with her. Should I tell her what I've done, and what I'm intending to do? Or should I let her believe that I am going to travel with Roberto, even though I will be left behind at home for two days before I go. I gaze closely at her while she glances at her cell phone, searching for something. "Hey, wow, take a look at this!" she pulls her chair closer and shows me the screen of her new Samsung. "Do you know what this is?" She stares at me, studying my face with such intensity it is like her eyes are boring into me.

"A house with a garden and tennis court?" I guess, shrugging my shoulders. She holds the phone closer, as if she wants me to eat it, and yelps excitedly.

"A house? Hello? Take a closer look! That's Conley's place! He lives in the Hamptons. And this is just ONE of his places. There's no justice in this world." Luckily she has taken her cell back, and seems to be searching on Google Earth for injustice, because she murmurs to herself, "We're crammed in, six of us, in an apartment with three floors, and he is on his own, and I'm sure every evening he has at least one guest, and probably doesn't even know what room to use first. You should visit him in New York. You can send Robby off to do his own thing!" We both laugh, as I try to strike a sexy pose, with my belly.

"Hello Mr. Conley," I say, making my voice sexy, "have you been shooting one of your action movies today?"

CHAPTER 23

"There is a God, and he obviously loves me! Hallelujah!" Susie throws her hands in the air when Frank and Ken come into reception at Coney Island Hospital. Ken stops, a confused expression on his face, before Frank shoves him forward, a grin on his face. They go straight to Susie's desk, while she leans forward expectantly, her eyes sparkling behind her glasses. "Tell me honey, where have you been hiding this cutie? Is he even legal?" She lets her glasses fall, to dangle on their chain, as she makes a show of looking Ken up and down, before reaching out her hand. "Hello Kenneth, I'm very pleased to meet you! I'm your Dad's crazy friend, Susie. Unfortunately, your old man hasn't told me very much about you. You know how it is, there isn't much time for talk when we get together!" She winks at him and lovingly slaps his hand. Ken looks amused.

"Susie, at last!" he replies, "My father has told me so much about you! It's an honor to meet you in person!" He takes her hand and kisses it. Susie's mouth slowly opens, her eyes gazing at Ken, then slowly going to Frank.

"Frank, I'm sorry, but it's over! I want the younger version of you. It looks like quite an upgrade!" Frank's laughter fills the reception, as he once more appreciates Susie's extrovert nature and sense of humor. Then the elevator door opens and Dr. Shilling, dressed casually in jeans and a turtleneck, comes striding out. He is heading for the exit when he notices the two men at Susie's desk from the corner of his eye. He recognizes Frank and changes direction to say hello.

"Mr. Conley, it's nice to see you again! I'm heading out, I'm afraid, I should have rang you to ask when you were next coming in. Have you told him?" He smiles at Susie, who makes a show of shaking her head, pretending to be shocked.

"I would never give hospital information to strangers!" she says, and blinks at Frank and Ken. Frank's gaze moves from Susie to Irish Coffee and back again, thinking for a moment how this is all taking so long.

"We have good news, we have made progress with the patient in INT7." Dr. Shilling smiles at Frank like he is offering him the role of a lifetime. "She's awake!"

Frank's heart starts beating faster. "Linda's awake?" he hears himself say the words really loud, as if he is trying to shout above the noise of his heart. Dr. Shilling looks at him in confusion, then shoots Susie a questioning look, softly saying a single word, asking a single question, "Linda?"

Susie tries to explain. "He gave the victim in INT7 a name. Isn't it pretty, Linda? We'll soon find out if it fits well with her real name." Dr. Shilling nods and turns back to Frank.

"Yes, Linda is awake and she is capable of understanding what is said to her. She hasn't said anything yet, but it is still excellent news, don't you think? As I said, I have to go, will I see you tomorrow?" This is obviously a rhetorical question, because he is already striding away to the sliding doors at the entrance.

Frank turns to Susie and gives her a wide-eyed gaze. First she grins at him, then at his son. "Well, will you take a look at our superhero! He's speechless, and he can't stop grinning at me!" Ken laughs heartily and looks at his father.

"Hey, Dad, this is great! Linda is really on the mend! Would you prefer to go up alone? I'd completely understand, And I don't mind staying here with Susie." She immediately squeaks in joy.

"No, no, come with me. I don't know if I should be glad or worried. What am I going to say to Linda? And I can't really keep on calling her Linda, otherwise she'll..."

"Relax, sugar! You should be glad! Linda's awake, it looks like she's a fighter, to survive everything that's happened to her, and now you can go and greet her, and say hello! Everything else will take care of itself."

"Does she know what her body had to go through? Is that why she isn't saying anything? I don't know what I'm going to say to her, Susie. I don't want to be the bearer of bad news, and Dr. Shilling just left! No, I can't do it!" Frank buries both hands in his hair, glancing from Ken to Susie, and back. Ken puts a hand on his agitated father's shoulder, gives him a loving pat and digs in his fingers.

"Come on, dad, Susie's right, let's go and say hello to Linda, and welcome her back into the land of the living. There will be another doctor on duty, and you aren't allowed to answer her medical questions anyway. For now, all you have to do is be a friend. And who knows, maybe she'll recognize you, and give you a hard time about the way you read!" He winks at Susie, as he goes to the elevator.

CHAPTER 24

Roberto sits in silence opposite me, in a train compartment we have to ourselves. It used to be that there was hardly ever a pause in our chatter. I have really messed everything up. The irony of all this hasn't escaped me. I have given up my breast in the name of what we wanted for our lives, my entire body in fact, but my husband is hurt and furious because I made the decision about my own body for myself. He's punishing me with the silent treatment, but very soon there will be two of us. My pregnancy is so far along, and I'm in great shape. There are less than two months to go, and I have made it through every problem. Almost every problem. But I will have to get through this alone, and deal with the consequences. I've always been good at prioritizing and sticking to my priorities. I'm logical in my decisions but when I act, it's on what my heart wants. It's always worked very well.....up to now. Like Roberto said, I've always had an advantage over him....

"Hey, look at the size of the line at the economy counter. Is everybody going on holiday today?" Roberto seems to have forgotten his upgrade for a second, but then he winks at me and goes over to the counter with the words Business/First Class on a screen above it, with a spring in his step. It looks like he is really looking forward to New York and to seeing Simon. If I didn't have my own ticket for two days time, I would probably start sobbing. I hold my belly with both hands, and stroke the places where there is movement. They say that the baby can feel all the emotions the mother feels. I quickly think about my own upcoming holiday, and all the great excursions I'm going to go on. I've never traveled alone before, but these thoughts still make me feel better, after all, I'm not really alone. I've learned quite a lot about people's character over the last few weeks, how open-minded, curious and wonderfully helpful strangers can be to somebody who is obviously pregnant.

I smile at Roberto as he takes his boarding pass and comes over to me and the baby, who has now fallen asleep again. He takes my hand, and I enjoy his touch the whole way to passport control, where our paths will part for a couple of days. "Okay, so I have to go the rest of the way alone." Roberto is fighting back tears. "I'm so sad it had to be this way. I wish I'd thought again, and said you could come with me. It won't be the same without you, we've been together so long. And I'm going to miss this bump." I move closer to him and hug him, my bump between us. Has the time come to drop my bombshell?

"Do you really mean that?"

"Of course I mean that! I'm so sorry. After so long together, you deserve better than this! Who am I to say you can't go on holiday?" He squeezes me to him as best he can, and I can hear his heart beating fast.

"Okay, I'll take care of it. You know I can't say no to you!" I slap him on the ass and say casually, "Okay, I'll see you in New York real soon! I'll get a ticket somehow." Roberto's eyes go wide, and he grins at me in a way I haven't seen in a while.

"For real? You'll try?" We share a long kiss goodbye and I think, Jasmin, you really got away with it, and now you can also play the heroin! I feel like I'm floating on air on the train journey home. I feel so relieved, simply happy for the first time in a long time! The first thing I'll do is add another person to my booking for the helicopter trip, and book another ticket for the musical. If I'm lucky, there will still be a seat in my row.

My cell vibrates and I see a message from Roberto, "Big Apple and Daddy are waiting!! Hurry up and book, and please forgive me! I was an idiot!" My heart melts. I've finally caught up with him, and at last we can enjoy our dream together!

CHAPTER 25

If riding the elevator was an amusement park attraction, today would be a blockbuster day at the Coney Island Hospital. Frank moves from foot to foot, while the elevator stops at every floor. Doctors and nurses come in and press the button for the very next floor. Frank wonders why they are all wearing trainers, if they take the elevator for just one floor. Some people get in, notice that it is going up, and get back out. The journey up seems to be taking forever today, and Frank sighs out loud. "Almost there, Dad," Ken whispers to him, and then there is a ding as they arrive at the fourth floor, the ICU. Apart from one nurse, they are the only ones to get off the elevator to be left feeling like they are free floating. Frank slowly heads toward INT7 looking round wildly as he goes. "Are you looking for somebody, dad?" Ken seems to be keeping a close eye on his father, and Frank suddenly notices that his son still has a reassuring hand on his shoulder.

"Yes, Leslie, the nurse. I would really like to talk to her first." Almost as soon as it is said, he hears his name, "Mr. Conley?" spoken by a male voice he is not keen to hear. He looks down slightly, into the small, distrustful eyes of Officer Tropman. He stares at Ken then looks back at Frank.

"Hello, we've been waiting for you. Both of you, please follow me into the waiting room. There are a couple of things we need to talk about." He gestures in the direction they should go with a uniformed arm, trying his best to feign a smile. Ken almost has to shove Frank, to get him moving. His serious son, with his deep respect for the law, pushes his action-hero father into the waiting room that is to be the site of the interrogation. Frank stays by the door, remembering all too well the last time he talked with the police here. He folds his arms in front of his chest, waiting for the questioning to start. The police officer sits in a chair, and motions for the two Conley's to do the same. The obedient son immediately sits, the hesitant father stays on his feet with a shake of the head. He notices that there is another police officer in the room.

"Mr. Conley, I assume Dr. Shilling has talked to you on the phone, and has explained what has happened?" To avoid wasting precious seconds with Linda, he quickly nods. "Excellent. And who are you?" he asks Ken, who answers clearly and helpfully.

"Kenneth Conley, Mr. Conley's son. I'm a lawyer." Frank is surprised by this answer for a moment, but he's sure Ken has a good reason.

"Okay, pleased to meet you. Let's start. The victim in INT7 has today awoken from the medically induced coma. We aren't allowed to talk to her yet, because she isn't answering questions, in fact she isn't speaking at all. Dr. Shilling thinks that there is a possibility that she might speak to you. I'm told you've been spending a lot of time with her over recent days and weeks. Do you know the victim, Mr. Conley?" Tropman once again seems to be suspicious of him, and Frank glances at his lawyer, Ken, his eyes pleading for help.

"No, my client does not know the victim in INT7. The first time he saw her was on Coney Island beach. She was injured and he arranged for medical assistance, which is why, along with feeling sympathetic to her plight, he has been visiting her here. He has dedicated a significant amount of his time to reading her stories and news articles, to tell her about himself and his life, and he was advised to hold her hand to promote a speedy recovery. He does not know all the details of her case and he has not been told the prognosis either. All he has been is a good Samaritan who was very moved by the unimaginable and horrifying events that have befallen this woman." Ken brings his short but heartfelt plea to a close by slapping his hands together and he looks over at his father who is about to burst with pride. The police officer is equally impressed, he glances at his colleague and gets up out of the uncomfortable looking seat.

"Okay, fine, Mr. Conley, if the victim tells you anything that might help us work out who she is and find her attacker, ring me immediately!" Frank, who still hasn't said anything, nods with eyes closed and unfolds his arms to wave goodbye to the police.

Frank slaps his son triumphantly on the shoulder, as Leslie appears in the door a smile on her face. "Hello Frank! And you must be Kenneth! Nice to meet you, I'm Leslie." She waves them both forward and grabs Frank by the arm when he gets close enough. "Okay, quiet now, let's go in and see Linda! I'm sure she's waiting for you. She won't talk to us, poor thing." She shows Frank to INT7.

"What is she doing? I mean, Dr. Shilling said she can hear what's happening, but can't speak."

Leslie looks at the two Conleys and her voice suddenly becomes very professional, "I'm sorry, I sometimes forget that not everyone is used to this sort of thing. Okay, Linda has awoken from the deep sleep that Dr. Shilling put her into. She woke up earlier then we were expecting, she seems to be a real fighter. We took out her breathing tube, she can breathe on her own now. Her eyes are open and she is looking round, a little shocked and confused, but that's to be expected. She has a cocktail of drugs in her system, because of the pain, so she's very subdued and breathing very lightly. Her eyes react to movement and light, which makes us think she can see what's going on and understand what is said to her. We still don't have any idea why she isn't speaking. There is no damage to her vocal chords. Now we are just waiting to find out if Linda is a little Diva, and she will only talk with the creme-de-la-creme." She winks at Frank and gazes at him as if she is waiting for him to give her the okay.

Frank looks at Ken and says, "I think I'll go in alone."

Ken nods that he understands, "I'll just stay in the waiting room and treat myself to a delicious cup of hospital coffee. Say hello to Linda for me, and tell her I'm looking forward to meeting her." Frank puts his hand on the door handle and takes a deep breath, before leaving the room.

CHAPTER 26

All the windows are closed, the TV is unplugged, and even the bed has fresh sheets for our return. My suitcase is only half full and I have a small, practical carry-on bag when I go out into the street and wait for the taxi that is going to take me to the airport. The last two days have been packed with examinations, errands, tying up a few loose ends and researching all the contact numbers I might need in case of an emergency connected with my pregnancy. Dr. Dubois has also been doing research and has even found a few contacts at Coney Island Hospital, where Simon works. He has told me several times that he still doesn't like it that I am traveling, especially as I have been losing weight. My results aren't good and I could go into labor early. The only thing I am interested in is whether everything is okay with my baby. I am perfectly happy as soon as I know that and I secretly think, 'There are doctors all over the world, and they have babies in every continent.' But I'm touched by his concern and I feel sorry for him that he has me for a patient. I decide to write him an email every day, so he can forget about me and get on with the other babies he has to deliver.

I feel like a star in business class. I have a lot of space for myself and my belly, I can lie down to sleep, there is a little wall between me and the next passenger, and I even have a menu to choose my food from. It is worth the price, and I'm glad that Roberto also had the opportunity to travel this way. Today I'm sure I'll be well rested and fresh when I get to New York, despite the long flight, and I'll be able to dive into the hustle and bustle of the big city. First I'll do a little shopping, which is why I have left plenty of space in my suitcase. They say the shopping is fantastic in New York, and I have already researched some shops for maternity clothes. I'm also planning to buy some new shoes and a nice handbag. I also have a lot of other things on my 'to do' list. I have to visit some restaurants and museums that Claudia has recommended, along with the usual sights. I'm also sure that Simon will have some plans for things for us to do together. He's been living in New York for a while, after all, and he'll know a lot of places only the locals know. I snuggle into my bed, with socks and blanket provided, and let classical music transport me to the land of airplane dreams.

As we are stars, or just because we have paid more, we can leave the plane before anyone else. Claudia, who has traveled a lot, has also warned me about immigration. There are a lot of questions about where I'm coming from, where I'm going to, and why. Everyone coming into the country is under suspicion. The line behind me is like a python that is about to burst. How many of them want to make a new life in the land of opportunity, never to return to their homeland? I don't know if I could ever emigrate and start again somewhere new. So far away from everything familiar to me, my family, my career, my friends, my language and the excellent quality of life in Switzerland. But so many do exactly that, but why? Is it because they are running away, excitement, for their career, or just for a change? I have to ask Simon about this, and whether he will ever go back.

I'm looking forward to them both welcoming me, as soon as I have finally gotten my light suitcase off the carousel. It appears just as I am thinking about it. As fast I can, in my uncomfortable support stockings, I go with the flow of people heading for the exit. So many faces with smiles, looking for loved ones, happy, and excited. Here tears of joy at being reunited, jubilant embraces and hungry kisses there. I look round the press of people for Roberto's face, but I can't see him. I emerge from the crowd, go past the tour guides holding signs with the names of their group and travel agency. I still don't see my husband.

CHAPTER 27

Frank hears Linda's rhythmic heart beat, and also sees it on the screen beside the bed. He can also hear his own heart, just as loud, but wilder, more erratic. He sees Ted sitting at the foot of Linda's bed, eyes glassy as he looks in her direction. Frank hardly dares to look at her face, even though he has waited so long for this moment. He slowly goes to his chair at Linda's hand and silently sits down. He looks at the monitor, at the heartbeat he knows so well, then his eyes move until they are looking at Linda's face. Her eyes are closed, and it is the first time he sees the face without a tube in its mouth. The nose and cheekbones are still hidden behind dressings, where they were broken and repaired. Her mouth looks swollen but Frank can tell she has full and well formed lips, and he wonders if her teeth have been damaged, or if they have had to be replaced. Her closed eyes look like they are drawn in the face, long, dark lines at the base of long, black lashes. Frank has never seen such long, curved, full lashes, without the aid of expensive cosmetics. Today, he can see her hairline, they must have changed the bandages on her head. She has a high, shapely forehead and dark hair. Frank thinks, 'She looks like a natural beauty, with hair the same dark color as her eyebrows and lashes!' In his business, he could never tell if the women he worked with kept their natural hair color, or if they even knew what it was anymore.

"Okay, Linda, where were we? Ah, here's the parking ticket I left as a bookmark! My forgetfulness can be expensive sometimes." He looks at the woman in the bed, still deeply asleep, her breathing heavy, and starts to read from a copy of 'The Picture of Dorian Grey' by Oscar Wilde. As soon as Leslie comes in, he will get Ken. He reads, "He looks at his beauty in the mirror." As he draws breath at the end of the sentence, his gaze falls on Linda, who is looking at him with big, dark green, twinkling eyes. He feels a shiver run down his spine and his voice fades away. They both look at each other for a moment in silence, before Frank collects himself and gently says, "Hi, welcome back."

She seems to smile a little, or at least the edges of her mouth twitch and her eyes narrow slightly for the briefest of moments, before they close for a second, perhaps a way of saying thank you. It falls to him to make conversation, because Linda is just staring silently at him. Her deep breathing and her having to close her eyes for long seconds at a time seems to Frank a sign that she is in pain. What does she know about the state she's in and about what happened to her? Has Dr. Shilling told her everything and that is why she is silent, given over to pain and sorrow?

"I'm Frank, Frank Conley, and I'm very pleased to see you awake. I hope it's okay for me to talk to you like this?" Her eyes briefly close again, followed by a deep sigh. "Are you in pain? Do you want me to ring Leslie for you? She's the friendly nurse..." Frank automatically puts his hand on Linda's as he asks this question. He feels the hand below his slowly move away. He starts to snatch his hand away, ashamed of touching her so thoughtlessly, when she puts her beautiful long fingers on the back of his hand. He is deeply touched by this ordinary and hardly perceptible gesture, and he looks her thankfully in the eye. He pulls his chair a little nearer, but he doesn't know what to do or say next, to avoid ruining this magical moment. He hardly dares to breathe as he feels Linda's finger lightly tapping against his hand. He looks at her hand and watches her slightly lifting her index finger. He wonders if this means anything, or if it is just some kind of reflex.

The door opens and Leslie comes into the room, "Is everything okay with you two?" She gives Frank an expectant look. He shakes his head, almost imperceptibly, but then replies.

"Yes, everything is going fine so far with us. She's awake. I think she's in a lot of pain, and she often takes a sharp breath." She moves her index finger again just then. Frank is now sure she's trying to speak with him. He looks in her eyes and asks, "Are you answering me with your finger?" The index finger taps. He turns excitedly to Leslie and says, "She's signaling with her finger!" Leslie quickly hurries round the end of the bed to join Frank, and looks at the two hands on the bed.

"This is amazing! Are you in a lot of pain?" she asks Linda.

"Yes, she is," Frank answers.

"Okay, then I'll get a doctor. Good work Frank! Hey, you know your son is still in the waiting room. Should I ask him to come in?" Before Frank can answer, Linda taps on his hand with her index finger.

"Good idea, I think somebody wants to meet him." He looks at Linda with joyful eyes, as she closes her own eyes and breathes deeply, "and please tell the doctor to hurry, Leslie, she really is in a lot of pain." Linda's eyes stay closed, but her hand strokes the back of his a single time, and Frank knows this is to say thank you.

Leslie has hardly left the room before Linda opens her eyes and Frank sees a tear flow down her cheek. "Be brave, the doctor will be here in a moment, and he'll give you something for the pain." He softly strokes the skin of her cheek with his left hand, and he feels tapping on his right hand again. He looks down and sees that her middle finger is moving. "It's not just the pain, is it?" Index finger. He thinks about how it is important to phrase his questions well, to avoid confusing her. "Is there anything else you want to tell me?" Index finger. "Do you know who did this to you?" Middle finger. Obviously not, Frank thinks, who would know such a monster. What does she want to say to him, how can he find out her name this way, not to mention why she isn't speaking, as he has been told her vocal chords are undamaged...

CHAPTER 28

After waiting for an hour, ringing Roberto's cell number without any reply and going half crazy with worry, I call a cab to take me to the hotel where I have the booking which I luckily haven't canceled. After the few weeks I have had, I wasn't sure if it was really for the best for me to stay with Simon, too. I didn't consider whether Roberto would stay with me at night, it wasn't my main concern. At least he knows that I have a room at the Marriott in Times Square, and he didn't comment when I told him. He was so pleased at my being able to book a seat at such notice, it seemed he didn't take much notice of such details, Now, here I am in a New York yellow cab, and I can no longer hold back my tears. What has happened? Something must have happened, because this was so unlike Roberto.

The taxi driver keeps glancing in the mirror, worried, and eventually asks, "Is everything okay, lady? Do you want me to take you to the nearest hospital?" I silently choke back my sobs and think about what a fright I must look, though a New York taxi driver probably sees much worse than me every day.

"Thanks for the offer, that's nice of you, but I'm okay. It was a long journey and I will be glad to get to bed in the hotel." I am surprised how easily the English words come to me, even though I haven't used the language for quite some time. Apparently you don't lose skills you learned in childhood, like riding a bike.

I don't notice much about the drive through New York. The flight has been more difficult for me than I thought it would be. Roberto not being there to pick me up at the airport is bothering me, and I can't help imagining the worst. He wouldn't be the first tourist to disappear without a trace in this huge land. Not Roberto, please not him! I start to sob noisily, causing the driver to give me a concerned glance in the mirror.

"Is everything okay?" he asks. "You really don't look too good. I can take you to the hospital if you want, lady!" I instantly calm down, and reply in the most professional voice I can muster. I can't help but ask him a question that is eating away at me.

"Do you know how many people disappear in New York? My husband wasn't at the airport to pick me up. Should I go to the police?" I grab the back of his seat with one hand, and keep the other on my stomach, as if this gesture will make me feel better. The driver bites his bottom lip, watching the traffic while he thinks about how to answer.

"Shit, I'm sorry. Leaving a pregnant woman at the airport, that's really bad! But I'm not sure the police will be

in a hurry to help. When was the last time you saw him?"
He keeps glancing at me in the mirror, most likely because
he's afraid that I'm going to give birth right there in his cab
and that he will have to assist with the birth.

"It was back home in Switzerland, but we exchanged
messages yesterday, when I gave him the time my fight
would arrive. Why wouldn't the police help me?" He turns
onto a side street, then another, before bringing the taxi to a
halt.

"Hotel Marriott, Times Square, here we are. They
won't start looking for anyone until at least 24 hours have
passed. Check-in to your hotel, and who knows, maybe he's
waiting for you inside, and all this is just some mix-up. I
sure hope so. I mean, to hell with him if he did this on
purpose! Good luck!" He gets out of the car, opens my door
and helps me out. I'm glad of his assistance as I get to my
unsteady feet on the busy street in front of the hotel. I glance
at the meter and get some money out of my purse to pay
him, including a generous tip for causing him such worry.
My suitcase is already on the sidewalk and I give an
exhausted nod of thanks, and smile at the first New Yorker
I've met on this trip. An employee comes and greets me as

soon as I enter the modern lobby. He takes my light case and accompanies me to reception like a faithful dog.

***

I run myself a bath, and I can hardly hear the water for my own sobbing. This can't be happening! I pace backward and forward, agitated and in pain, in my beautiful bedroom, with its comfortable looking bed and a breathtaking view. I feel miserable and I'm hoping that the bath will at least ease my physical pains a little. Once again, I pick up the phone and press zero. "It's Steiner, still no messages for me?" I am expecting them to say no, and that's exactly what they do, just like the last time, three minutes ago. Another New Yorker who thinks I'm crazy, and is probably wondering how I even managed to get through immigration. The bath is ready to provide a moment's respite, and I take off my clothes. I put one foot int the bath, then the other, and I start to relax a little as I smell the lavender drops I brought with me. I slowly sink into the water and close my eyes. Silent tears flow down my cheeks, and I only faintly hear that somebody is knocking at the door...

CHAPTER 29

The painkillers given to Linda by the doctor on duty work quickly, and Linda's eyes look more awake and alert. She is not breathing so deeply anymore, and it feels to Frank like she is squeezing his hand tighter. Ken and the doctor come into the room together, and they both stay at a distance, in the corner of the room. Ken listens intently to Frank telling the doctor his latest experiences with the patient. He looks at Linda and is aware of the trusting and hopeful way she is gazing at his father. The way she is looking at Leslie and the doctor seems fearful, or even distrustful. She uses her two fingers on Frank's hand to answer every question the doctor asks, never taking her eyes off him. Ken remembers a documentary he has seen about rescued animals who refuse to move from the side of their savior, and growl at anyone else, or even bite them. They trust only this one person, only allowing themselves to be fed or touched by them. 'These last five minutes in INT7 are just like the documentary,' Ken thinks, his lawyer's brain going over thousands of possible causes. The doctor looks annoyed about this development and nods to Leslie to leave, before they both go out together. The door has only just closed when Linda looks over at Ken and smiles. He takes it as an invitation and moves closer to the bed, where he stands beside Ted and says a friendly, "Hi, welcome back. I'm Ken, Frank's son." Linda smiles again, and a tear rolls down her cheek. Frank holds her hand tighter and glances at Ken in confusion. The clever and caring lawyer looks at Linda's dejected face and slowly says, "Do you understand us?"

"Of course, she understands us," Frank says, shooting him an irritated glance. "She has been answering questions for the last ten minutes." Linda's middle finger taps on Frank's hand, and he turns to look at her in shock. More tears are flowing from her big, green eyes, her gaze helpless. "Linda....oh I'm sorry, I gave you that name because I didn't want too keep saying 'woman' or 'victim'....so, is he right, are you having trouble understanding everything we say?"

Frank feels a firm touch from her index finger on his skin. "Do you have pain in your ears?" The question is mostly intended as rhetorical, just to be sure this isn't the problem. He feels her middle finger. "Linda, shit... Please forgive me..." Her index finger. Frank looks at Ken in surprise. Is she saying yes about Linda or to his apology?

The door opens and Leslie enters. "Okay, gentlemen, it's getting late, visiting hours are over, and they have been for a while and this woman needs to rest. I think there has been a lot of progress today, thank you very much Frank! We can at least ask the patient how she feels, and make sure she has everything she needs for the night." Linda's eyes look at Frank, pleading for help, and he seems torn. His son comes to his assistance again, as Ken moves over to Leslie.

"Leslie, seeing as none of her family are here, and my father would like to take on this duty, wouldn't it be better for the patient if he spends the night here? It looks to me like there is already a level of trust here, and a certain amount of acceptance. I'm sure that the patient would get well even more quickly, if you would call Dr. Shilling for us?" Ken looks at Leslie, who is giving him a skeptical, but also an understanding look.

"I can see why Susie is so taken with you! Well, okay, I'll call Dr. Shilling." She winks at Frank, and speedily leaves the room.

As if they have to savor the last few minutes, in case Ken's intervention doesn't work, they both give the frightened woman in the bed their full attention. Ken takes over the conversation for his action-hero father, who is easily distracted. "Is your name Linda?" he asks, even though he is pretty sure he knows what the answer is going to be. Two pairs of Conley eyes stare at Linda's hand. No reaction. Frank takes a Kleenex from the box on the bedside table and dries the tears from her face.

"Hey, this has all been a lot to deal with. Everything is okay. There's no need to cry, we... I... am here. And I'm sure Dr. Shilling will let me stay here overnight, if that's what you want?" Index finger. "That's great. Do you recognize me?" Index finger. "My face?" Index finger. "My voice?" Index finger. Frank looks at Ken and feels sure the coma patient really is understanding what is going on around her. "Do you like the book I have been reading you?" Index finger. "That's great, we'll read some more in a second, as soon as we are alone again, okay?" Index finger. Frank sees Linda's face relax a little at the distraction and he knows exactly what question he will ask next.

"Guys, Dr. Shilling has agreed to allow Frank to spend the night at your bedside." She nods and smiles at

Linda, "if the patient agrees." She looks at the index finger, waiting for an answer. "Okay, I'll bring you another blanket and a cushion. It won't be particularly comfortable, I have to warn you, Frank." She turns to Ken, "You, my silver-tongued friend, will have to leave with me. We don't want the young lady to be overwhelmed by too many charming gentlemen." She motions to the door and gives him time to say his goodbyes. Ken goes to Linda's bed, slowly strokes her forearm and gently squeezes her hand.

"Bye, I'll be back to visit soon, if that's okay with you?" He sees her index finger tap on Frank's hand and smiles thankfully at her. "Good night! See you soon!"

"I'll be back in a second, I promise!" Frank says, and gets up. He gently pats her hand and goes out with Ken into the corridor. Leslie pats Ken on the shoulder as he goes by.

"Well done," she says, then disappears behind a filing cabinet into another room. Frank hugs his son tight!

"Thanks, son, you're one of a kind and I'm very proud of you!"

"Any time, dad! Take things slow, she's frightened, very frightened! You're all she has left now, and I'm afraid also all she has from her past...."

CHAPTER 30

It's so beautiful here! I have never seen such an amazing sunset. The colors that the sun is bringing out all around are better than in any picture painted by an artist at their easel. The wide expanse of the sea and the relaxing noise of the waves entice me closer to be able to feel it stronger. I float in the water, and I have the feeling of being weightless in the warm water that gently surrounds me. A warm breeze carries me toward the ever brighter light of the sun, deeper into the red and far away from the sound of the waves. I feel my lightness, rising up, my weightlessness. All my worries have gone, along with my fear and pain. An indescribable feeling of endless bliss and deep contentment washes over me, and I feel like I want this explosion of sensations to last forever. I see a gray cloud on the far horizon, and I paddle away from it with all my might, toward the light, nearer to the warmth and freedom from worries. The cloud takes the shape of a giant hand, pointing at me, seeming to reach for me. It darkens and approaches. It is bringing a storm with it. It sucks me inside and I am thrown around and shaken. I feel terrible unease and pain.

"Jasmin! Jasmin! Can you hear me?" The cloud seems to be speaking to me, but I can't see it. I don't want to look at it, I just want to escape it, to return to the warm light of the weightless, pain-free zone. "We're losing her, she's losing consciousness! Again, now!" The dark cloud shoves me away, then immediately pulls me back to its painful reality. "Damn, there's no time! What are you doing? Are you crazy? You can't do that! You'll kill them both!" Indescribable pain makes me scream and I open my eyes, terrified! A white coat, a hand pushing my mouth closed with a cloth that stinks so badly of chemicals I can't think. A last look into the familiar eyes that are looking back at me, mournfully and full of worry. They seem to want to comfort me, to give me hope, and to say goodbye.

The deep sleep will help me recover and give me strength. I dream of Roberto, our child, our apartment in the city, I look at the skyscrapers of New York, speak to the intimidated taxi driver, talk to Claudia on the roof terrace, wave hello to my mother, close the door to the office of professor Kunz, give the Swiss Air flight attendant my boarding pass, give the porter at the Marriott a friendly smile, play 'Fuer Elise' on our piano, hand out the graded tests to my pupils, float a candle in a creek, kiss Roberto at the altar and see the smiling face of Dr. Dubois alongside a monitor showing a 3D image of my unborn child.

The sea has become rougher and the storm is building. It comes closer, waves breaking threateningly. The warmth has gone, leaving only cold behind, attempting to spread to every part of my body like a parasite. Only the heat in my belly, in my face, and in my breasts is able to resist. It burns and presses at my skin, leaving ashes and emptiness behind. It slowly gets into my lungs, and I try with all my might to cough it out! I can hear a rattle in my throat, and I want to scream out the indescribable pain, but all I hear is a whimper. Something tender and cold touches my burning face and the sea talks to me. It pities me, it comforts me, it wants to care for me and it strokes moisture over my face, again and again. It makes me weightless, then gently lies me on something soft, gently touches my hand, holds my wrist and takes away my pain...

CHAPTER 31

After less than five hours of restless and uncomfortable sleep, Frank is gently awoken by the vibration of his cell phone in the breast pocket of his rumpled shirt. He slowly opens his eyes, then it takes him a moment to work out where he is. Linda's deep breathing and closed eyes remind him how quickly she fell asleep, and how they couldn't 'talk' anymore. She was exhausted and upset after the few hours of wakefulness. There is a question that he was dying to ask, but he read Oscar Wilde to her instead as she slept. His neck and his back hurt, after sleeping in such an uncomfortable position during the night, and his mouth feels like a dry sandstone cave. Leslie warned him, and she was right. He will have to ask her for some toiletries, so he can freshen up, then get an extra large mug of coffee from the canteen. If Susie hasn't forgotten that he is at the hospital, she will definitely leave him a doughnut from her breakfast.

"Hello Tom, good morning." Frank stops his Blackberry from vibrating and stretches his arms and legs by going over to the window. "Yes, I'm fine. I spent the night at Coney Island Hospital, in fact I'm still here, you woke me up.....Yeah, right, she woke up yesterday and we are trying to find a way to communicate with her. She's very upset, she'll need more time...... Yes, I'll do that, why do you ask?....Today?....Dammit, I forgot.....What time?....No, no, that's fine, I'll go there, too. Can you find something nice for me!" Frank laughs and he notices Linda move, but then fall asleep again. He speaks softly into his cell phone, "Okay, I have to go.....no, she's asleep, but my bladder is bursting....I'll ask Ken to take over for me here. I think it's important that one of us is here with her, something isn't right. I'll tell you more about it on the way to the children's home, when are you going to pick me up? .....Can you bring me some clothes, I can change here......I don't know, you're the manager. Something that will be okay for reading fairy tales to the kids. ....Okay, thanks! Hey, what do you think, can we take Freja along? ....cool, okay, I'll see you at one!" He hangs up, puts the cell phone on the table, glances at Linda to make sure she's okay, then goes into the room's bathroom.

"Frank?" He hears his name called loudly from the room. Linda? He quickly finishes freshening up, washes his hands and pushes his wet fingers through his unruly hair to try to tame it. He immediately goes through to the main room and looks at Linda's bed. Before he has a chance to feel too disappointed, Leslie goes past him and is quickly busy with the hoses and drips.

"Good morning sunshine! How was your night? Did you manage to get any sleep? The nurse on duty here in the night said you talk in your sleep, did you know that?" She is chewing mints, and Frank can't help feeling jealous.

"No, I didn't know that. I hope I didn't use any harsh language." He grins in Leslie's direction. "I think she was asleep all night, at least as far as I remember. We read a little more of our book, but we didn't talk any more. She drank a lot of water and then she soon went to sleep." Leslie checks the monitors and makes notes in a small book.

"Very good. I see she was given some pain relief around three, and it seems she was awake. Sleeping beauty on the chair was fast asleep and missed it." She giggles gently and this confirms Frank's suspicion that Leslie and Susie must be good friends.

"Looks that way, Leslie, have you got a toothbrush I can use?"

She presses a few buttons, turns a dial on a drip and looks directly at Frank. "It's probably a good idea that you get out of this room for a while. Go see Susie, get a coffee and some fresh air, it's a wonderful morning and the sun is shining. Dr. Shilling can visit the patient while you're out, I'll freshen her up a little and the bed too, and put a toothbrush in the bathroom for you. I can put a razor with it and some cologne, if you want?" She smiles at him, takes him by the arm and leads him to the door. "You'll come back with new strength to talk with her some more. Dr. Shilling will wake her for her morning check up, and I'm sure he'll want to talk to you and to her. Say hello to the old battleaxe at reception for me, and tell her to go easy on the doughnuts. Maybe she'll listen to you!" She closes the door behind them, after Frank glances one more time at the sleeping Linda.

Loaded down with coffee and a fruit shake, Frank goes through reception to Susie's help desk. She is siting in her chair, concentrating and shaking her head at what she is reading. Frank stops in front of her and he looks down at the magazine on the desk. Above a picture of him and Ken at the entrance to Coney Island Hospital, is written in big letters, "Action Hero and his Lawyer Involved in Brutal Murder Attempt!"

CHAPTER 32

Claudia is lying, with a green face mask on, on a couch at her regular beautician. She has been treating herself to this since she turned 50. Neither she nor her family are sure it actually helps, but a woman needs a few luxuries. The hour and a half of face pampering, the comfortable steam, and the wonderful smell of the lotions and creams give her a moment of pause during her active month, and also give her the feeling she is something special. It is a way of spoiling herself and enjoying her time. It is something she has had to learn how to do. Four children will make a wife forget that she is also a woman. Without stereotyping, she is a hundred percent certain that any woman would enjoy the same treatment. The good feeling lasts at least until her front door opens and her everyday life brings her back down to earth. She has sworn to herself that when her children are no longer financially dependent on her, she will visit the hair stylist every week. Even if it is just to have her hair washed and nicely styled.

"Do you want a couple of magazines to flick through? That mask will have to stay on for 20 minutes. Your skin is very dry, but that's just how it is at this time of year." While her favorite beautician is saying these comforting words, she puts a stack of magazines in Claudia's lap. "The new Gala is in there, the latest gossip from Hollywood. It's a good issue, you'll see!"

CHAPTER 33

"Holy shit!! How can you be so calm? This stinks to high heaven? Who even writes this shit anyway?" Susie rips the page out of the magazine, balls up the paper and throws into the bin below the desk. She grabs the rest of the magazine and turns it over. "I'm going to write an email to the editor! There must be an email address here somewhere, or are they too frightened to print their contact address!" Frank reaches over the desk, calmly takes the gossip magazine from her hand and throws it into the waste basket along with the rest of it.

"You shouldn't even read that trash, Susie. Not even half of what they print is true, and they make the picture look either worse or better, depending on how the reporter is feeling that day. You'd be better spending the money on doughnuts! And, talking about doughnuts," he smiles at the still fuming receptionist, "have you got one left for me?"

Susie gives Frank a pensive look from behind her reading glasses, bites her lower lip and lets the glasses fall to swing on their chain. She turns on her chair to a bench behind her, picks up a small box of doughnuts, turns back and places it carefully right in front of Frank. With her hand on top of it, she slowly gets up from her chair and leans toward Frank.

"And now Sugar Mama wants to hear exactly what happened in INT7!" She taps the box with her finger, a little like the way Linda has been doing with Frank's hand over the preceding hours.

"Holy mother of god, Frank, what are you doing down here stuffing doughnuts in your face? Get out of here, go up to her and find out what happened to her!" The tears in Susie's eyes combine with her words to show just how upset she is.

"Leslie told me to take a break. Besides, she's having her check up, so there's no reason for me to be in the room." Frank jams the last chunk of sweet pastry into his mouth, and has to wash it down with a swig of coffee. He doesn't dare to say anything right now, but he decides that he will some time tell her how he can't understand how she can eat this crap every day. He briefly closes his eyes and gulps the rest of the doughnut down, then takes another couple of sips of coffee.

"Leslie, that skinny snake! I bet she said something to you about me eating too many doughnuts?" She turns to the desk and lifts the receiver. "Speak of the devil! …..it's none of your damn business how many I've eaten. My incredible sexy curves need them." Susie winks lasciviously at Frank, who is shaking his head. "Yes, is he jealous? ….okay, I get it, I'll tell him! And hey! Both, young and old are for Susie, got it?" She puts the receiver down, picks up the empty box from the counter and pats Frank's hand. "Irish Coffee is waiting for you in the sick bay."

Frank writes a text to his son in the elevator, and asks him to stand in for him with Linda from one o'clock. Even though he isn't sure why he's doubtful, his clever son doesn't hesitate to help. He immediately gets a short, informative and supportive answer back.

Frank puts his cell phone back in his pocket, and he notices that there is a card in there. He pulls it out and glances at it, and he remembers the police officer asking him to pass on any developments. Officer Tropman, something is off about him. Frank can't put his finger on it, but he just doesn't trust the man. He decides he will have to talk to Tom about it, to see if he has any contacts at the police department. Frank would bet his Aston Martin that this guy is who is leaking to the press. It wouldn't be the first time a dirty cop went looking for some way to make some extra money.

The muscular action hero slowly and cautiously opens the door to INT7. The curtains are closed and Frank isn't sure what he is going to find inside. A hesitant step into the room and a new vista is revealed to him. Dr. Shilling is beside Linda standing in his white coat, slowly lowering her arm back down to the blanket. Linda's head has been unbandaged, revealing her face. She is sitting up in bed and her long black hair is falling on her shoulders. Frank can see the woman in the bed well for the first time, a very beautiful woman. "Mr. Conley, it's good you are here!" Irish Coffee comes over to Frank and firmly and enthusiastically shakes his hand. "Come over, the patient has just woken up, the bed is freshly made and she's had her check up. She's a real fighter, I can tell you. Just look at the color that has already returned to her face! You have to tell me which book you are reading to her, it has had an amazing effect in such a short time!" The flood of words from the excited head of medicine is too much for Frank.

"The Picture of Dorian Grey, by Oscar Wilde," he stammers in confusion.

Now it's Shilling's turn to be confused, then he smiles, "Oh, the book! Yes, a classic, I read it when I was young." He goes round the bed to the monitors and glances at them one last time. "Okay, that's good, I'm really pleased at the progress you're making, and how brave you are." His words are primarily intended for Linda, who has been looking only at Frank's eyes since he entered the room. Dr. Shilling sits in the chair beside her and moves a little closer to her. "You lost a lot of blood and Mr. Conley found you just in time. That's why I asked him to come here, especially as you will only to talk to him right now. That's fine, you can take your time. I'd like to take this opportunity to give you a little information about your condition. Do you think you're up to that?" his gaze follows hers to Frank, who is standing frozen at the end of the bed. Linda closes her eyes, takes a deep breath, lifts her arm and holds her hand out to Frank, palm up.

CHAPTER 34

Claudia looks into Jasmin's office, to make sure she hasn't missed her. She doesn't seem to have arrived yet, everything is untouched, in the same place it was the day before. The folder of signed documents on the desk, the letters with personalized addresses in a tidy stack, and fresh flowers to welcome her back. Claudia hasn't ever looked forward to welcoming a boss back so much, but Jasmin has become more of a friend. And when the baby arrives, she'll have even more in common with her. Jasmin will make a good mom, she's sure of that. And with Roberto, her perfect husband, who supports her and loves her more than anything, she'll come through the health problems that life is throwing her way with flying colors, too. Claudia has seldom met a woman as strong and self-confident as her boss, but also so friendly and approachable. When is she going to be back? She glances impatiently at her cell phone to see if a message has arrived. She puts it back down on her desk in disappointment and turns on her computer.

"Van Thiel? ...Hello Mr. Kunz, Mrs. Steiner is..." Claudia is interrupted by the director who asks her to come immediately to his office on one of the floors above. She slowly replaces the receiver and mumbles to herself in confusion, then gets up just as slowly and goes to the door. "Hung up ...what the devil is going on here? ...what do they want with ME?" Before she leaves the room, she turns on her heel and reaches for her note book and a pencil. She takes the stairs, as is her habit, whatever building she is in, and walks up three floors. She has to rest a moment to catch her breath and straighten her blouse. She takes one more deep breath and enters the office of her colleague, the assistant to Professor Kunz.

"Hello, Claudia, don't bother to wait, just go on in." The woman, who is usually a hard ass, seems to be in a good mood. Claudia isn't used to being spoken to by her in such a friendly and caring way, and it instantly makes her nervous and apprehensive. She knocks on Kunz's door and enters without waiting for an answer. She opens the door to reveal the most elegant room in the entire school.

"Please take a seat!" Professor Kunz tells her, as he waves at a leather chair. He rises from his chair and goes to a globe on a table. He opens the globe to reveal a small bar, much to Claudia's surprise. It is full of shot glasses and bottles of schnapps. She can hardly breathe, watching every movement of the most senior person at her school, eyes wide. He picks up two glasses in one hand, opens a crystal decanter and pours dark liquid into each glass. The whole operation seems to take forever and Claudia has the feeling she might pass out if she doesn't exhale soon. What is there for the two of them to be celebrating? What is there that is worthy of a toast between the strange combination of Professor Kunz, the school director, and Claudia Van Thiel, a future head of school's assistant, Jasmin? It has to be about Jasmin, there isn't anything else that could have caused this strange performance to take place.

"There you go, Single Malt," the school director says, as he hands one of the crystal glasses to the still speechless Claudia, then he sits in the leather chair opposite her. He glances at his full glass, and turns it in his hand as if studying the cut glass. "You have family, don't you, Mrs. von Thiel?" He doesn't raise his eyes to look at Claudia, and she seems about to lose her self-control. Her answer is a little brusque.

"My name's VAN Thiel, and yes, I have a large family. Four children and my husband. There's also my mother, my step-parents, and-" The professor lifts a hand to apologize.

"I'm sorry, you must be nervous. This isn't the way I usually do things." Claudia wonders what he means by the way he does things. Does he mean the way he asks assistants to come to his office, shoves a whiskey into their hand and then attempts clumsy small talk? Claudia places the glass on the coffee table that is positioned between her and the man she is in this strange conversation with. She puts her notebook and pencil down beside it and quickly strokes her hands over her thighs before folding them in her lap.

"Professor Kunz, may I ask you why I am here, why you are giving me a glass of whiskey in the middle of the day, and why you are asking about my family?" She looks directly at the gray-haired man and raises her eyebrows to emphasize how suspicious she is of the situation. He puts his glass down on the glass table, holds it at the top for a second, as if making sure he has put it down securely, then drops back down into his seat.

"I'm not good at passing on bad news, especially when it has come like a bolt from out of the blue."

CHAPTER 35

Dr. Shilling touches Linda's arm comfortingly for a moment and gazes into her sad eyes, which can't hold back the tears any longer. "I'm so sorry, but I promise you we will do everything possible here and give our all to get you back on your feet, so you can carry on with your life. I'm an optimist, but I'm not the kind of doctor who makes empty promises! As soon as we have found your family, everything will start to get better. A lot of support and having somebody by your side will give you new energy. And it looks like you have made a new friend. That is a great start. I'll leave you two alone and, Mr. Conley, could you please let me know if there are any developments." He quickly squeezes Linda's arm and nods to Frank before he goes. He stops by the door for a moment, then turns and tells him, "Officer Tropman was here today. We sent him back to the station, told him the patient isn't strong enough to talk yet. Just so you know, in case he calls you." Frank can see that he is also suspicious of the police officer, even though he adds, "I suppose he's only doing his job, and we all want to know who is responsible.... but there are limits here at my ICU, and he is going to have to learn that, that pushy..." he opens the door, which swings out of the frame with a click, and then Frank and Linda are alone.

Linda can't stop crying, her tears accompanied by soft sobbing. Frank goes round the bed, picking up the teddy bear as he goes, and he pulls a Kleenex out of the box on the bedside table. He gently places the bear by Linda's shoulder and, for the first time, sits on the bed so he can be closer to her. He gently dries the tears from her face.

"It's okay, let it all out," he says, gently, his words caring and comforting. "That's better. They say tears are the language of the soul, and that they purify the heart." He reaches for a new Kleenex, but Linda's hand holds him back. He puts his hand below hers in the now usual way. "Are you in pain?" He gazes at her, waiting for her answer. She gulps audibly and her mouth slowly opens. Her tongue emerges and she dampens her dry lips. Frank's apprehension intensifies and he wipes away another tear, so that he is doing more than just staring at her. His eyes rest on her mouth, which closes again before she swallows loudly one more time. "Are you thirsty, Linda?" His face moves closer to hers, as if trying to see the answer in her beautiful eyes.

"I'm terrified..." she whispers, her words loud and clear. Frank leans back away from her in shock and surprise.

"What?" he stammers. "Say that again." He wants to make sure he hasn't imagined that Linda just spoke to him, and not with her fingers, with her voice.

"I'm terrified, Frank!" Frank works hard to hide his excitement at what she has said, and tries to concentrate on what the words might mean, and he is thankful for his years of working as an actor.

"Why are you so terrified? Let me help you!" She closes her eyes, as if she is trying to squeeze out the last of her tears. She sighs and gazes at the man who saved her life.

"I don't know anything!"

Frank gets another Kleenex and dabs at the last few tears on her face, he gazes at her pensively. "You don't know who did this to you? Can you remember anything?"

She shakes her head, wets her lips again, and sighs. "You don't understand, I don't remember anything!"

Frank can't help but notice how slowly she is speaking, almost syllable by syllable, and he offers her a glass of water with a straw. "Here, have a big sip of water, your throat has to be very dry." She does as he suggests, taking sip after sip. She falls back onto the pillow, pain written in her face as she squeezes Frank's hand with all her strength. She closes her green eyes and her voice is almost a whimper.

"I don't know who I am!" Frank's eyebrows arch and his eyes narrow. He again leans toward her face.

"Do you know your name," he whispers, and Linda barely perceptibly shakes her head, "Do you know where you live?" She opens her eyes and her face is so near that Frank can feel her warm breath. Her gaze is endlessly sorrowful.

"I don't know a thing. I don't even know what I look like..." Frank's head slumps forward for a moment, then he looks into her beautiful face again and tries to work out, among his whirl of emotions, how he feels about her.

"We have to think clearly now. You don't remember a thing. No memories at all. Not your name, not what you look like, not about the events that brought you here. We have to tell Dr. Shilling this right away, Linda, he'll know what to do, I'm sure of it!" Frank already has his finger on the button above the bed when Linda gently holds him back.

"I know that I don't think in your language, and that I don't understand everything you say. I definitely don't understand everything Dr. Shilling says, but he frightens me. His white coat frightens me." Frank suddenly notices that she has a slight accent but he also notices how she is using some difficult English vocabulary.

CHAPTER 36

Claudia is frozen in place on the comfortable leather chair, staring at Professor Kunz. She takes a deep breath and reaches for her glass then pours the whole lot, burning, down her throat. She grimaces then her face relaxes a few seconds later, as she hands the glass to the man opposite her as if she is a child with a broken toy. "Can I have another, please?" She gazes at the director, eyes blank, and he quickly gets up, takes the glass from her, pours a little more into it and gives it back to her without saying a word. He slowly sits back down in his chair with a deep sigh, and he also takes a sip of his as yet untouched drink. He looks at Claudia, his head inclined.

"Did you know about how ill Jasmin was?" The question is not asked in a reproachful tone, he just wants to know more about what is going on. Claudia's second single malt whiskey is burning in her throat and she closes her eyes in order to enjoy the comforting effect of the golden liquid. First she simply nods, then she opens her eyes and looks at the glass table.

"Yes, but she didn't think her health was so bad. She was in such a good mood, and she didn't believe things wouldn't turn out all right for her."

Claudia slowly climbs the many steps to the loft, in her hands she has a lot of bags ready to be filled. She feels like an intruder as she turns the key in the door, opens it and goes into Jasmin and Roberto's apartment. She smells the aroma of lemon grass, and she even thinks she detects a hint of Jasmin's perfume. She has to fight back tears, and she quickly tries to think of something nice. As she tries to think of beautiful memories, she takes off her coat and shoes and takes the empty bags straight through to the bedroom. Standing in front of the large wardrobe she remembers the first time she met Jasmin Steiner. The enigmatic beauty of the lecturer, much too young to be doing that job, who through her ambition, her directness and her loyalty quickly won the respect of everyone on the team. Claudia was skeptical to begin with, but that soon passed when she took the minutes of the first session Jasmin chaired, and from then on she always assisted her with admiration. She had seldom been treated as an equal by a superior, and been so supported as she had been by Jasmin from the very first day. Claudia can't imagine how she is going to carry on without her pregnant and joyous boss. She takes out one item of clothing after the other, folds them carefully and fills the bags she has brought with her.

Claudia's cell rings in her purse, which she has left out on the stairs. She runs past the rows of bags in the corridor and pulls out the phone. "Van Thiel?" She is breathing a little heavily and sits down on the stairs.

"Hello? Who is this?" She hears a crackling that she recognizes from the international calls she makes.

"Roberto? Is that you? Helloooo?" She hears the phone being hung up. She looks at the display of her cell phone and pushes the call back button. She hears a different ring tone to the one used in her country. She is about to hang up when she hears a man's voice.

"Claudia? Can you hear me?" It is definitely Roberto. Claudia has never felt so happy to hear his voice, but at the same time it feels like a dagger in her heart.

"Roberto! Yes, it's me!" She can't hide how unhappy she feels any longer, and she sobs into the Samsung. "Why did this have to happen Roberto? Where is she?" She can hear how bad the reception is and she presses her cell closer to her ear.

"I have really bad reception here, I'll phone you back later, I promise, from a landline! Hey, Claudia, thanks so much for all your help! I appreciate it! I don't know how I could organize all this without you! I don't know if I heard you right, were you asking where Jasmin is now?" Roberto's voice has calmed Claudia a little, and she remembers how Jasmin used to talk about how much she liked it. Without waiting for her reply he says, "She's still in the hospital for some last tests."

She waits for him to add something else and then breaks the silence, "Roberto is it a boy or a girl?"

CHAPTER 37

The morning coffee is making itself felt in Frank's bladder, and he stares at Linda. "I have to quickly go to the bathroom, I'll be right back. I have to get rid of the damn coffee from this morning, okay?" He winks at her and puts his hand on the bed. "Don't go anywhere!" He grins and walks by her bed, watching her nod and close her eyes.

He flushes and zips up, and he hears the door to the room open, and he tries to hear if anyone says anything. He notices a toothbrush, still in the packaging, some toothpaste and a small bottle of cologne on the wash basin, and he glances at the bathroom door. "Leslie, you angel," he murmurs, and he unpacks the toothbrush. He drops the toothbrush as he is trying to open the toothpaste. "Ah, damn!" he grunts. He hears quick steps in the next room, and the door to the corridor opening and closing. He puts a lot of toothpaste on the brush and puts the fresh tasting blob in his mouth, then he hears a loud beeping from the room. He quickly pushes the door open, sees that Linda's eyes are still closed, and that she is lying pale and limp on the pillow. The monitor beside her is blinking and beeping threateningly. Frank immediately throws open the door to the corridor, looks round, then yells, "Leslie! Leslie quick!

Hello! Is anyone there?" Leslie is there in a few seconds, along with two other people, all coming running from different directions, and they push past him to get to Linda's bed. Dr. Shilling comes a second later and hastily shoves Frank to one side.

"Her blood pressure is falling. Quick, adrenaline and Propofol!...Intubate!" The monitor is still beeping, but now much more feebly. Frank runs a hand through his hair, the other hand is holding the toothbrush so tight he might break it. He can't see Linda, just Dr. Shilling's tense back and Leslie's concerned face.

"More adrenaline!" Dr. Shilling's usually calm demeanor is gone now. Suddenly the monitor starts beeping, the doctor's body relaxes, and Leslie's sigh of relief means there is good news. His throat is tight and he stands motionless at the door. "She's back! That was close!" Dr. Shilling turns to Frank, his gaze questioning. Frank looks at Linda's face, and sees her color returning and he is slowly shaking her head.

"I was just in the bathroom for three minutes, and the loud beeping started when Leslie left the room." The doctor turns to the nurse and then back to Frank.

"Leslie wasn't here, Mr. Conley, we were both with another patient. What made you think she was in here?" Frank goes slowly to the chair, puts the toothbrush on the table and rubs his face with both hands,

"Well, I took a leak, and I heard the door. I heard it again when I was brushing my teeth. I figured it was Leslie, coming to check on the patient, or something. I have never seen anyone in here apart from you two!" Dr. Shilling frowns at Leslie.

"You didn't tell anyone to come in here, did you?"

Leslie shakes her head and her pale face looks at Dr. Shilling then Frank. "I'll call security!"

Frank looks at her trainers as she runs out into the corridor, and he remembers the steps he heard. "It was a man," he mutters to himself.

"Sorry? What was that, Mr. Conley?" Dr. Shilling is standing in front of the monitor, nodding pensively. Frank stands up, looks at Linda, then at the door, and he stares at the man in white.

"The person who was here, he must have been a man. I heard his steps, and they were nothing like when Leslie left the room just now! Everyone on this level moves around like you are walking on clouds. I noticed that from the first time I was here. The person I heard wasn't from here, and weighed more than Leslie. The steps were men's!"

Dr. Shilling comes to stand in front of Frank and he thinks about how seldom somebody is able to look him directly in the eye. The tall doctor suddenly doesn't look as motivated and positive as he did just an hour before. "Did you see anyone in the corridor, or did you hear anything else?"

Frank shakes his head and turns in Linda's direction. "No, nobody said anything, not a word," he bites his lower lip and wonders if Linda would also forget this.

***

Frank is being asked a lot of questions by security when his son gets off the elevator. He looks happy at first but that look is replaced by a serious expression as he strides toward Frank being interrogated out in the corridor. "Dad? What's going on?"

Frank puts his hand on Ken's shoulder as a sign to wait a few moments, and finishes with the words, "That was all that happened, gentlemen." The security people go off in all directions and Ken gives his father a concerned look. He takes Ken by the shoulder and takes him into INT7 and closes the door behind them. "Kenneth, something weird is going on here! I think Linda might be in danger!" Ken notices how nervous and agitated his father is and pours him a glass of water, in the glass next to the unused toothbrush.

"Here, drink this, then tell me all about it." The lawyer passes his father the glass of water and looks at Linda. "Oh, that's good, it looks like she's doing a lot better. There are no bandages on her face or her head anymore, and no tubes." Frank slowly drinks, also looking at Linda's face.

"Ken, I think the monster intends to finish his work!"

CHAPTER 38

Claudia has been given the whole day off, so she can deal with Roberto's business, which means Jasmin's business. Her SUV is now full of bags of all shapes and sizes. She is driving through the busy streets of the city center, out to the area where the biggest home for asylum seekers for miles around is located. She has never been to it, but Jasmin had often told her about it when she took her old clothes there, and about the people she met and the interesting conversations she had. Thinking about Jasmin was painful and she had been asking herself since the conversation in Kunz's office what this terrible event meant for them all. The parking lot at the entrance is completely empty. There are no visitors for the asylum center. It must be difficult to get to know people in a place like this. Claudia parks her car right in the middle and walks to the entrance with purposeful strides.

"Hello, I rang earlier, Van Thiel, about the clothes." A short and friendly woman, plump in a knitted cardigan and linen pants comes over.

"Hello. It's nice of you to come visit us! You're a friend of Jasmin Steiner?" Claudia nods and quickly changes the subject.

"Is there anyone who can give me a hand? I could use some help. I have a lot of bags out in the car." She points through the glass door at the big SUV, with bags piled so high they are obscuring the windows.

"Oh, that's wonderful! All size 6, with maternity clothes, right?" It is intended as a rhetorical question, and she immediately continues. "I'll send a couple of strong young men right out, and they can take it all to be sorted. It'll just be a moment. We'll be right with you." The short friendly woman disappears round the corner and Claudia thinks about how funny it is that this woman has found herself the perfect job.

***

She drives back to the apartment in an empty car and goes through the list she got from Roberto about what is to be done today. Jasmin's clothes are now all given away and her jewelry packed up for her mother. It's impossible to imagine what she went through with this terrible turn of fate. 'A silent farewell ceremony!' were Roberto's words. But there was no Jasmin to say goodbye to. How horribly disfigured must she be, that she can't be buried in Switzerland.

Claudia can imagine that he does not want to return to the same apartment, with all the memories, everywhere he looks. But to turn his back on his homeland, that she can't quite understand. Of course she's happy for him because he has found a position in a hospital in New York so quickly. Obviously, even looking after children is much easier for working parents, and most importantly less expensive than in Switzerland. But would Jasmin have wanted her child to grow up in America, seeing as she was so integrated into the Swiss education system herself, and a proponent of its quality? She doubted it, and has to accept with a heavy heart that there is no point bringing up such issues. She stops at a red light and watches a family cross the street with a small child in a baby carriage. She wonders what Jasmin's young baby looks like? She has to remember to ask Roberto for a photo of Miriam.

CHAPTER 39

Frank is reluctant to leave Linda after the recent frightening event. She is still sleeping as he leaves INT7, in a fresh change of clothes. Ken comforts him by telling him he will stay with her until he gets back from story time at the children's home outside the city. A security guard has been put on the door until the police have finished taking statements and then he will be replaced by one of their people. Frank already has a queasy feeling when he thinks about being questioned by Tropman again. With Ken there, this will be respectful and only about a limited range of subjects. First however he will have to urgently tell Tom about it.

"Okay, tell me all about it old boy! What is going on?" Tom is sitting, looking in Frank's direction in the back seat of the Mercedes and raises his eyebrows quizzically. Freja is comfortably nestled between them, enjoying being back with her owner, with her head on his leg. Frank shakes his head, closes his eyes and leans his head back in the comfortable seat.

"Tom, it's a nightmare that Linda has been through. I can't put into words how sorry I feel for her, and I also feel so helpless! I can't remember what I told you last... where did we leave off?" His eyes are still closed and he feels his body slowly relaxing.

"She woke up and was making signs with her fingers. But you haven't told me what horrible thing happened to her, to leave her in this state!" He looks expectantly at Frank, who is calming down. The storyteller in the light gray suit and light blue shirt takes a deep breath, opens his tired eyes and looks pensively out of the window. He collects his thoughts for a moment, before looking directly at his manager, a man of the same age as him.

"I'm sorry I can't tell you everything. Linda has lost her memory, and can't remember a thing. Not even her name, what she looks like, where she comes from, or what happened to her. That last part is a blessing, of course, because nobody should have to remember something like that. The only thing that is clear now is that English isn't her native language so she doesn't understand everything. But she speaks very well, which means she has lived here a long time."

"Wait a minute, wait a minute, how do you know she speaks well? I thought she was making signs with her fingers!" Tom looks at the actor in confusion.

"She spoke for the first time this morning, shortly after I talked to you on the phone. Then the head doctor was with us and told her all about her condition when she first came in. It was obvious that she didn't understand everything, but I couldn't ask her exactly what she had missed. Then her attacker came looking for her and tried to kill her."

Tom shakes his head in disbelief, "Sorry, what?? While you were there? And you just blurt that out, Frank, so casually? There is obviously some stone-cold killer running around, with his sights on this woman, who you are currently paying more attention to than that dog you love so much, and you're just telling me this now? We have to make sure you're safe, right now, and arrange for bodyguards round the clock!" He hurriedly pulls his cell phone out of the breast pocket of his jacket and is about to dial a number, when Frank takes it from him.

"Not yet, Tom, please. It will attract too much attention and I want to keep the whole thing as protected as possible. The latest news from the gossip magazines has been plenty. I have a suspicion about who the leak could be. How good are your contacts in the NYPD?"

Chapter 40

Director Kunz is in Jasmin's office, looking round a little lost. "We took out an ad, and we've contacted selected employment agencies. We'll find somebody internal for the position of head of school, even if none of the other candidates are quite right. Mrs. Van Thiel, could you clear out Mrs. Steiner's personal things, and remove her files from her computer?" He goes to Jasmin's desk and opens a drawer, lost in thought.

"Yes, of course I can do that, when do you need the office done by?" Claudia takes a step into the room and for the first time takes a good look at it. 'Jasmin had a great eye for interior design,' Claudia is realizing this for the second time, after having thought it while clearing her apartment. Everything was in just the right place, whether it was vintage, antique or very modern, she made it fit, as if she had designed the room around the details. This space isn't just an office, it is a refuge for a smart woman who wants her work space to be as comfortable as home. She hopes her future boss will also feel at home here, and won't feel the need to change everything. At least she's sure it will be a woman who will be running the department.

The small tin with all the passwords is in the lowest drawer. Claudia opens the vintage tin and remembers how happy Jasmin was when she gave it to her, after finding it at a flea market. "Look at this Claudia, it's perfect for my passwords! I doubt anyone will ever need them, but I bet nobody has ever packed up passwords so beautifully before." She remembers it like yesterday, the assistant looking at the boss in the doorway, holding up the little package. And now the moment has come when these passwords will be needed after all. She opens the tin, and the password to unlock the computer is on top. Claudia starts up Jasmin's computer and waits, her fingers tapping on the desk until it asks her for a login. She carefully types it in and waits again. A smiling Roberto appears on the desktop. All the important folders are arrayed around his handsome face. Claudia puts a pen drive into the computer and starts sorting the folders. The folder marked 'private' is the first one she moves to the pen drive. She feels the brief temptation to open it, but she resists.

A good hour later, the dutiful assistant contacts the company's IT department and tells them they can do a reset of Jasmin's computer. It's the first big step that means Jasmin really won't be coming back. Claudia plays with the pen drive, then puts it in her handbag after a few minutes thought. She spends the rest of the day sorting through the folders in the filing cabinets. Jasmin had neatly put her initials on her personal things. This makes it easy to put the books that belong to the school on one pile and put Jasmin's in another. She will send an email to Roberto tonight, to ask what she should do with the things from the office. They hadn't gotten round to talking about that in their last conversation, because the nurse had called him over to Miriam in the incubator. She's a strong fighter, Roberto said. She weighs 2,000 grams, and she is breathing unassisted, so he will definitely be able to look after her unaided soon. He sent Claudia a picture of the small baby. Her dainty little hands covered her face protectively, as if she wasn't quite ready to be presented to the audience. But tears come to Claudia's eyes at the sight, wondering if she will ever meet Miriam? At least she is obviously in a very exclusive and therefore probably very good hospital, judging by the parquet floor to be seen through the sides of the incubator.

CHAPTER 41

With a lot of happy shouting, the children say goodbye to their superhero and wave excitedly at his car as it drives off. Frank and Freja are visibly exhausted by the two hours, but the storyteller enjoys the relief that the time with the excited little children have given him. "We have to do this again, Tom. I haven't experienced so much power, energy and joy for years. That one with the red hair, what a character! She's going to drive the guys crazy! What was her name?" Frank looks at his Manager, who is equally exhausted.

"Saskia," is his short answer, as he smiles.

Frank slaps his thigh and turns his attention to the driver, "Lou, I want to make a short stop at Idlewild in Brooklyn, before we go to the hospital. They should have plenty of books in foreign languages. We have to find out as soon as we can what Linda's mother tongue is!"

While they drive through the streets of the city with at least eight million inhabitants, Frank thinks about how strange it is to call a country a motherland, and to call a language a mother tongue. He leaves his fellow passenger in the car and goes directly to the bookstore. The action hero has hardly opened the door before a keen shop assistant comes up to him with a smile on his face, "Mr. Conley, Frank Conley, what an honor, Sir! Welcome to Idlewild! Are you looking for anything in particular?" His loud greeting has alerted the few customers looking through the shelves, and Frank switches on the winning smile he uses for the fans, but he keeps his gaze on the man he is talking to.

"Hello! Yes, in fact I am looking for something in particular. To be exact, I'm looking for foreign-language books. I'd like one book from each language, if you have something like that?"

The keen book expert is now standing in front of Frank, looking up at him. "Wow, you're taller than you look in the movies! That's crazy!"

Frank puts a hand on his shoulder, because after all these years he knows how much people like to tell their friends that they have been touched by a star. "I'll take that as a compliment, my friend." He has just given him another little gift, intentionally. "So, what about it? How quickly can you get those books together for me?" The nervous looking and proud bookseller nods, tries to stay professional and disappears quickly among the bookshelves. Very soon there are a number of books on the counter, arranged in different stacks.

"Sir, these are all the different languages we have. This book is in French, "Le Petit Prince," a story about-"

Frank reluctantly interrupts the helpful bookseller, "Wow, that's what I call efficient! When I came in here and saw you, I knew you would be able to help, that you would know exactly what I want! Wonderful! You know what? I'm going to take all of them with me and look at them at home in peace!" Frank's new fan, who is unable to see any fault in the action hero, picks up the first stack of books, his cheeks red, and carefully puts them in a bag. He smiles at Frank from behind the bag, rings them up and absently clears his throat. The actor already knows the question that is coming, and he takes a pen from his breast pocket.

"Could you sign this...?" And there is suddenly a pad of paper in front of him with the book store's elegant logo. "Make it out to John!"

"The best bookseller in NYC! You were a big help John! Frank Conley," Frank writes in big curvy letters.

Frank gets into the back seat of his car with a big bag. Tom ends a call just as he gets in. "Tropman is clean, and an outstanding officer, who hasn't failed to close a case. He's very dedicated, because he wants to make captain, and he is a tough negotiator. We don't have to worry about him, even if he still wants your ass for what happened this morning..." Tom frowns and gives Frank a slightly worried look. Frank nods, lost in thought and pulls his vibrating cell from his breast pocket.

A message from Ken, "Let's meet at my place, I'm already here. Don't worry about Linda. Ken." Frank looks in astonishment at the display and reads the message again, before holding the cell for Tom to see, without commenting.

Tom frowns and gives Frank a quizzical look. "I thought he was going to stay with Linda until you got back!?" Frank knows that something must have happened, for Ken to be acting this way. His son, who is also his lawyer, never did anything without thinking about it, never did anything that didn't make sense. Frank thinks about how much he takes after his mother, and how proud Frank always is of him. He types 'OK' using the tiny keyboard of his Blackberry and tells Lou about the change of destination. He scratches Freja behind the ear and murmurs to himself, "He wants my ass..."

CHAPTER 42

Today they will be eating out together again. They do it once a month, that's the agreement Claudia has with her family. Since everyone always goes their own way, with school, work, hobbies and friends, they hardly see each other. Most days they just see each other as one is going in and the other is going out, as often with the bathroom door as with the front door. She is probably the only one who looks forward all month to this evening, even if she notices every time that they all enjoy telling each other all about their own lives, their successes and their experiences.

Torr, Claudia's husband, has become more distant over recent years. They don't really see each other very often, even though they are often together, in the house, at the same time. It's just that they both use the time to catch up on their personal interests. How often has Claudia realized that the children were the main duty of their marriage. Since they aren't needed by the kids so much anymore, they don't row as much, don't argue or fight as much. But now they will catch up with each other and what they haven't talked about before, or what they have almost forgotten about each other. He has always been a good husband and a father. She is going to make sure to spend more time with him. Depending on the new boss, she could reduce her workload even more, do the shopping and her chores in the time she would gain and spend the evening with Torr. She would even be happy to skip yoga and the book club to make the time. Jasmin's fate and Roberto's loneliness have shown her once again how important the relationship with your husband is. They have both definitely been neglecting that.

Today's restaurant has been chosen by her oldest. A cozy oasis, hidden away, that has some delicious Italian dishes on the menu. A small taste of Tuscany in the center of a Swiss big city. They get a table with a view of the courtyard, decorated with lamps and string lights. This must be an absolute refuge in the summer and is certainly perfect for festive meals. Claudia watches Torr and thinks that he still looks as good as he did 25 years ago. The sprinkle of gray in his hair suits him and his weekly visit to the gym has helped keep him in shape. She gently takes his hand and turns the wedding ring on his finger. The touch feels strange to him, and he gives her a confused look, "Everything okay, darling?" He still calls her that after all these years, even though she knows a lot of the reason is pure habit.

"Yes everything is wonderful, it's really nice here! A good choice, Mark! What shall we have?" Claudia picks up an old-fashioned looking menu and starts to hungrily look through it.

"Mom, is it true that Jasmin died in New York, and that Roberto isn't coming back?" Peter looks at his Mom while chewing pasta, and winding some more round his fork.

Claudia takes a big swig of her Chianti and nods, "Yes, unfortunately. She had physical problems and she went into labor much too soon. Nature decided against her, unfortunately. But she gave birth to a wonderful, healthy girl. And because everything is so terrible for Roberto, he wants to build a new life with Miriam. That's why I'm taking care of everything for him here." She makes sure to keep things brief, as she is talking, and not to go into too much detail. Alette, her youngest, still wouldn't understand everything. Claudia is keen to avoid the teenagers spreading exaggerated stories.

Mark gives his mother a serious look, "How can somebody just leave all that behind them? What about his job? His family?"

Torr answers for her and Claudia is surprised at how attentively he has been listening. "He was offered a good job at the same clinic where his friend works, the one who emigrated two years ago. Roberto has to find his feet and get everything set up. It is difficult to get past a loss like this, and people do it in different ways. It's impossible to imagine your mother suddenly not being there any more." He looks at his wife lovingly and continues, "But to be honest, I'm a little confused too about why he doesn't come back with Miriam, so he can say goodbye to friends and family. Did I understand you correctly, that her gynecologist can't get the autopsy report?"

CHAPTER 43

Ken is standing in the open-plan kitchen and makes his two guests a coffee with his French press. As always, there is a big bowl of water in front of Freja, and a bone. She grabs at the bone with her teeth and makes herself comfortable on her guest cushion, under the window with the breathtaking view of the city. "What do you mean they took Susie with them?" Frank goes to Ken's kitchen counter and leans on it. Not two steps behind him, Tom is standing with a look of confusion on his face. Ken grabs two cups from the cupboard and puts them in front of the two men. Then he reaches for a newspaper, not far from the cups, and puts it in front of the impatient men. He taps it with his index finger

"Officer Tropman seems to be a bit of a fan of gossip," he says. "He pressed this into my hands, after calling me out of Linda's room by saying my father should be more careful with his choice of lover! I want to see him at the police station immediately. Tell him that! For now, nobody is allowed to visit her anymore!" His face is a mix of concern and anger.

Frank and Tom read the headline, 'Murder Attempt for Love! Scorned Lover Seeks to Get Rid of New Love at Hospital! Who Will Conley Choose?' Below is a picture of Susie getting into Frank's limousine at the airport....

Frank throws the newspaper at the wall, runs his fingers furiously through his hair and yells a curse, "Damn, damn, damn! Not Susie! What the hell is this? I can't believe it! Who the hell publishes stuff like this? How is this even possible, after just four hours? It doesn't make sense?"

"Tropman was surprised by that too, and he thinks you're behind it, so you can get your face back in the papers. There's no such thing as bad publicity, dad! We have to get over there, they are going to put Susie through the wringer. Do you think she has a good lawyer?" Ken gives his father a comforting look and takes his cell out of his pants pocket, without giving his father a chance to shake his head. He dials a stored number and pours the two dismayed filmmakers a hot coffee while waiting for the person on the other end to answer. "Roger, Ken here. I need your help. Legal representation for a suspect in a murder case. A friend of my father's. He'll be paying the bills." He nods at his pale father. "Innocent, hand on heart! …. great! Half an hour at the 60th precinct, Coney Island NYPD.....at the entrance, okay. See you there!" The zealous lawyer puts his cell phone on the counter and goes toward the stairs upstairs. "I'm just going to change. Let's go! We'll rescue Susie from the claws of that cop and get to the bottom of this!"

***

In the passenger seat of the Mercedes, Tom phones the superior officer at the NYPD and tries to smooth the way. Frank looks at his son, still dismayed, "What is happening with Linda? How is she doing?"

"She slept a long time," Kenneth says, as he puts his hand on his fathers lower arm. "When she woke up she was shocked to see me and she asked after you. I told her about the attack, because she saw the security people at the door. They left the curtain open. She was in shock, but she can't remember anything. She remembers you went to the toilet, and that she was very tired. And that you spoke to each other. While she was speaking, she had the window in view the whole time, as if she didn't want to be caught talking to me. The head of medicine came by twice to check on us, and the friendly nurse came round a few times as well. Linda didn't say a word when they were there. Do you know why she won't speak to them?" Frank shrugs and his son, dressed in a dark blue suit continues, "Then everything started happening very quickly. Officer Tropman pulled me out of the room and asked where you were. Dr. Shilling and some nurses went into Linda's room and I found out that she is being moved for security reasons. But I couldn't find out where, we'll have to do that now. So yeah, and then I got this newspaper and everyone was gone." Frank's teary eyes look out the window at the busy city. He slowly scratches Freja's head and his thoughts revolve around Linda and Susie. The two women must both be so frightened right now, and he thinks about how much he would have loved to have spared them any danger...

CHAPTER 44

A month has already passed since Claudia was last relaxing in the hands of her beautician and she is enjoying this luxury today enormously. The last few weeks have been pure horror for her, even though she has kept trying to put herself in Roberto's shoes and to imagine how much worse it must all be for him. The apartment has been emptied and returned to the building management, the office readied for the new head of department and Jasmin's gynecologist is also, it seems, trying to get hold of the autopsy report, which is in New York. Now she can give herself over to mourning, and doesn't have to simply keep functioning. Her thoughts keep coming back to Jasmin's last hours. Claudia will have to ask Roberto for more detail when she gets the chance. She has the feeling that she has to fill in all the gaps in her knowledge, in order to be able to say goodbye to Jasmin. At the moment, there are just too many things that are unexplained and are bothering her.

"You have had a lot of stress recently? You look weary." The beautician gently strokes her temples and starts putting on the cooling mask.

"Yes, I've had a lot to deal with. My boss, and a good friend, died overseas, leaving a baby behind. I've been helping her husband to sort everything out here, because he doesn't want to come back." While Claudia, slightly sleepy, is saying this, the hand movements of the woman working on her are becoming slower as she listens attentively.

"That's terrible. I'm so sorry! Oh god, how horrible for the husband! Was she in an accident?" The cooling substance and the wonderful, calming aroma are already giving Claudia renewed energy.

"Yes, it's terrible for him. No, she already had physical problems, and she shouldn't have traveled so far in her condition." She doesn't go into detail, out of respect for Jasmin, and she sighs deeply.

"So, where did she go? Somewhere tropical?" The mask has now been completely applied, and is followed by some nice lip balm, so Claudia waits before answering.

"New York," she says, making the beautician, who is now standing beside her, suck in her breath.

"The things that happen there will make your hair stand on end! Do you remember the gala magazine and Frank Conley? The story goes on to get much worse. I have it here. Do you want to see? The mask has to stay on for twenty minutes."

"Give it to me, otherwise I won't know what's happening in the world!" Claudia says, as she nods and sits up straight in her chair, adjusting it to be a little more vertical.

***

On the way home Claudia thoroughly studies the Gala article. She decides to buy the issue at the next kiosk to be able to read it in peace and look at the pictures when she gets home. She can't describe the unease she starts to feel and the reason why. Probably the emotions are just stronger because of Jasmin's absence, because it was about the same city she had spent her last hours in, and where her body had been buried. Claudia stops in front of a rack of newspapers and magazines, looking for Gala.

"Can I help you?" the woman selling the newspapers says, looking out from between the chocolate bars and chewing gum, from in front of the cigarettes.

"Yes please, I'm looking for the latest Gala."

The woman purses her lips and inclines her head, as she points in the other direction to the one Claudia is looking. "Well, hon, if you're lucky, there's one left. They're over here." Claudia sees them now, a big stack of them. She thanks the lady and starts digging through the magazines. She's in luck, she finds the last one, and she lays it in front of the small glass window. She adds a packet of Mentos and a Peanut Butter KitKat.

"I found one! I'll take all this, please." She takes a purse full of receipts and loyalty cards out of her bag and gives the friendly kiosk attendant the money.

"Enjoy the Gala, and you'll see it's a good idea to only have one lover at a time, otherwise there could be trouble!" She winks at Claudia and there is no way she can know that it is just this article that will have such a big influence on Claudia and Torr's future plans.

CHAPTER 45

"Let me think … that must have been when he won his first Oscar. I noticed how stylish he looked in his suit on the stage. You see, his films aren't the sort that...." Susie's nervous flood of words is interrupted by the slightly wound up officer.

"You heard me, but I will repeat it, just one more time, Mrs. Manders. When and how did you get to know Frank Conley? This is no joke, lady. You should be taking the situation you're in very seriously! You are suspected of committing murder!" He slaps the table with the flat of his hand, making Susie jump a little, then she quickly regains her composure and hisses in reply.

"Oh, no kidding? And I thought you were looking for the next top model for the gossip magazines!" She takes a magazine from her handbag, which she has on her lap, then gives it to the police officer while she shakes her head. "You really shouldn't believe what they print in there, hon! Even if I say so myself, I look damn good in this photo, don't you think? Now I know..."

Officer Tropman is now visibly annoyed. He gets up, turns his back on Susie, lifts his face into the air and murmurs, "For the love of god, how stupid..." At the same moment the door opens, as if pushed by a ghost, and a man in a black suit carrying a briefcase enters the room, gently closes the door and calmly walks toward Susie.

"Mrs. Manders, pleased to meet you!" Before he can continue, Tropman interrupts him, resting with both hands on the desk.

"So you must be the lawyer?"

The lawyer takes his business card out of his breast pocket and slides it across the interview table. "That's right, I am. Roger Hard. Just like the way I negotiate." He gives the speechless Susie an arch grin and sits beside her. "So could you tell me why you are taking my client away from her important work in the middle of the day, and how you intend to say sorry to this fine and innocent woman? And why I have to find out from your boss that you have nothing against her apart from this gossip magazine." He taps the magazine on the table with the tip of his finger. "Please sit down, officer, we are both very eager to hear how you intend to explain this. And before I forget, your boss is in the next room, speaking to some very important people. Now, I'm sure he's asking all the right questions." Susie looks at the man in the suit beside her, then the man in the uniform opposite her, shakes her head, raises her eyebrow.

"Holy shit, I must be dreaming....." she whispers.

Frank is sitting in a small and dismal interview room, on the chair beside Ken, and he is looking straight ahead. He wonders how many criminals and even innocent people have sat in this chair, worried about their future. The door opens and Tom comes in with a smile on his face, accompanied by a police officer who is obviously of a higher rank. Tom sits down, while the officer shakes Ken's and Tom's hand in greeting.

"Gentlemen, I'm very pleased to meet you in person, even if it isn't in very good circumstances. Chief Officer Black. Tom and I have known each other for years." He sits next to Tom and crosses his legs. "I would like to apologize for Officer Tropman's overzealous behavior. He has not been very sensitive today, though I am convinced that he will help us get to the bottom of this bizarre case. It's very important to me that we work together, and so I would be very glad if you could keep me up to date with everything that happens at the hospital."

Frank notices his manager nod and he looks at his son. Ken can tell that his father is itching to ask a question. "Before my client gives you all the details he knows," he says, "we would love to know where Susan Manders is."

"Yes of course, sorry. She is sitting in the room next door, with her lawyer, as you already know. It is important that we find out everything she knows about what happened in the hospital directly, because I'm sure that she isn't allowed to tell you, even in private. I can assure you, Officer Tropman may not be very accommodating when he is working with members of the public, but he is not the problem here. I'm worried that we should be looking for the bad guy at the hospital. The only question is what is behind all this, and where this is all going. The receptionist might be the key. They see everything, have access to vital information and pick things up that happen every day. Mrs. Manders could help us crack this case."

CHAPTER 46

Torr comes home late because his advertising company has landed an account and he has to go through the details of the contract with his team, before it gets signed off on. Claudia is actually always pleased with him and proud of how motivated he always is and how dedicated he is to his work. He is one of the happiest people on Earth, doing his dream job. Where she can, she supports him, even if it is just listening to all his ideas and thoughts. Only this evening she wants to talk to him and share her inner unease. What is it about this article in Gala that she just can't shake. She seriously studies the article and repeatedly looks at the photographs. Frank Conley with a middle-aged woman, in front of a luxury car at an airport. Claudia doesn't know much about cars, but she knows from her son Mark what an amazing car it must be. The woman looks very natural and middle-class, and it is hard to imagine she is his lover, as the article claims. The second picture is in front of a police precinct and shows Conley with three men in suits with the caption, 'In front of the precinct with his lawyers and manager.' Why does he need two lawyers? And if his lover was in cahoots with him, why would they want to get rid of her rival? Claudia doesn't want to believe this gossip magazine, but the photo of the hospital with the caption 'Coney Island Hospital' keeps drawing her in.

What is it about this picture? She has the feeling that she has already heard these names, but she just can't place them. She closes the Gala and throws it angrily on the coffee table in her comfortable living room, picks up the remote control and starts zipping through the channels.

A far away hum wakes Claudia from her slumber. She hears her daughter's voice. "This is Claudia's cell, I'm Alette. ...Yes, mummy is here, wait a minute, I think she..." Claudia suddenly sits up straight on the sofa, gives Alette an angry look and waves at her with the cell phone in her hand.

"Van Thiel!" Her warning glare sends Alette to the floor above.

"Dr Dubois here, hello Mrs. Van Thiel. Please excuse me calling at this hour. Do you have a moment?" Claudia rubs her eyes, takes a drink of water from the glass in front of her and glances at the Gala which is still lying where she left it.

"Dr Dubois, yes of course! No problem, can I do something for you?" She has to clear her throat a few times and she feels embarrassed, typical when she is talking to the doctor on the phone.

"How are you?" The doctor's question sounds very sympathetic and honest. Claudia thinks to herself that she will have to change her gynecologist as soon as she can, because she realizes that Jasmin must have felt very comfortable with this doctor. Tears come to her eyes at the thought, and she knows that his question has flipped a switch inside her.

"Good question, Dr. Dubois, I don't know. I think I'm doing fine. Things have been hard recently, but in comparison to other people I really don't have any reason to complain. I really miss Jasmin, I mean Frau Steiner, and I still haven't come to terms with her loss. But don't ask me why. I just have a strange feeling in my stomach. Women, right? You're the expert, after all." Claudia is surprised at how many answers she has given to his one simple question, and she is embarrassed again at how pushy she is being. It is very doubtful he really wanted to know how she was when he asked her that question. It was most likely he was just being polite.

"From my years of experience with women, I can tell you that your feelings are very important, Mrs. Van Thiel! I'm absolutely sure that you have good reason that you can't put your sadness over Mrs. Steiner behind you. Take your feelings seriously, and explore them. I think women have a sixth sense and an incredible intuition, which I can rarely explain based on medical facts. But they can very often tell when something isn't right."

Torr quietly opens the bedroom door, so as not to wake his wife, and he finds her sitting at her laptop, her reading glasses on. For a moment he is a little shocked to see her this way, then he slowly goes over to her.

"Everything okay, honey? What are you doing on your laptop at two in the morning?" He glances at the bright screen and notices the logo of the Swiss airline. Claudia is concentrating, typing numbers and letters, hitting enter, then she throws her glasses on the bed. She looks at her husband with tired eyes, but she speaks excitedly, as if she has just woken from a restful sleep.

"Honey, how quickly can you get some vacation time?"

The tired adman looks in confusion at his wife, who seems to be losing it. "Sorry, what? You're planning our next vacation at this time of night? Honey, you can't be serious!" He sits exhaustedly down beside her on the bed and takes off his pants, socks, and pullover.

"Torr, look at me," and the attentive husband looks at his wife with her tired eyes, feeling just as exhausted as her.

"What is it, you nut?" he says.

She takes his face between her hands and presses her palms against his cheeks. "I need your help! We have to go to New York and we have to go as soon as possible! You won't believe what I heard today!"

CHAPTER 47

"Frank!" Linda's eyes are red and swollen from crying. She tries, painfully and with difficulty, to sit up in bed, but Frank is instantly beside her and gently puts his hand on her shoulders.

"Linda, no don't, lie down, everything's all right, I'm here now!" He sits on the edge of the bed right beside Linda, places his big hand on her cheek, and strokes her face with his thumb. "I'm so sorry that I couldn't prevent this. But I promise you I will do everything I can to put this monster behind bars!" The depth of his fury can be seen in the reddening of his neck, but he tries to give Linda a comforting smile. She puts her hand on his and closes her eyes in exhaustion. Her gentle sobbing is almost breaking Frank's heart and they sit in silence for a moment.

"I must have done something terrible, Frank. Do you think I'm a bad person?"

The sensitive action hero opens his eyes and looks again into Linda's sad eyes. "How in the world can you be thinking something so stupid? Of course you're not a bad person! You have just been through hell, and nobody deserves that. Whatever is behind what happened to you, we'll find out, and whoever did this, we'll make sure they end up behind bars. Look, I brought something for you, these will help us get to the bottom of this!"

He stands up and gets the bag full of books. He reaches in, takes them out, and spreads them on the bed, one after the other. While Linda opens a book and tries to read the first few sentences, Frank picks up his Blackberry and dials a stored number before being connected to his son a few seconds later.

"Hey dad, I just wanted to call you. The police have released a statement to the press and cleared Susie of any wrongdoing. They also said the victim would be moved to another hospital, without naming any names. Instead of calling you an insatiable lover, they are now calling you a hero. Tom has already been warned that he should send any requests for an interview to me. Depending on how far you get with finding out what language Linda speaks, there might be something useful to add. We first have to decide what our next step is. The important thing, dad, is for Linda and you to inform Dr. Shilling that Linda can speak and that she has lost her memory." Frank watches Linda and nods with the phone to his ear, listening to what his brilliant lawyer has to say.

"Does Susie know that Linda is being moved because of the press?" For a second he has the feeling that he has seen a look of surprise on Linda's face at what she sees in one of the books, the Little Prince. "Is Susie even back at the hospital?" Frank asks, as Linda closes the book and picks up another.

"No, she took the rest of the day off, to get over the shock of being interviewed by the police. But she'll be back in reception tomorrow, her usual bouncy self, and do exactly what Roger and the police tell her to do. She was exceptional today, dad! Tell her that. And Tropman was like putty in her hands after the interview, and he promised to bring her a box of donuts for breakfast, as an apology for all the trouble." Miles away, Frank could hear that Ken was laughing, and he only half heard the last few words his son just said, because Linda was reading one of the books.

"Ken, I'll ring you back. Thanks son!" He hangs up the call, puts the Blackberry on the table and walks slowly over to the bed, and sits on the edge.

"I can read this language. I understand everything!" Linda looks at Frank, her face brightening a little, and she holds the book out to him. It has a reclining woman on the cover, as if in a medieval painting. "It's called Perfume by Patrick Suskind." Linda's accent sounds so foreign to Frank, although he finds it wonderfully exotic. "And this one," she points at the one about the prince, "is called Le Petit Prince, by Antoine de Saint Exupéry." Another beautiful accent, that he knew well from when he did some filming in Paris.

"That's French, a beautiful language, especially when you use it....wow Linda, you know a lot of languages!" Frank is astonished and impressed, he gazes at her, as she opens another book, this one written in Italian, and reads some of it out to him, closes her eyes for a moment and looks at him.

"I understand all these languages, but the one that feels most familiar is the one from Perfume, but..." She opens Perfume again, reads out a few sentences and slowly closes it, then says disappointedly, "They aren't the words of my thoughts...."

"Hey, this is good progress!" Frank says, trying to make her feel better. "Now we know that you speak perfect French, Italian, and whatever language Perfume is written in! That's great Linda, hey what language is that?" He taps the book with his finger and Linda reads on the back that it is published in Germany.

"It's German. Do I have a German accent, or a dialect?" She opens the book again and reads a few more sentences. "Frank can you do me another favor, before we tell Dr. Shilling?" She gives the man who saved her life, the only person she knows, a beseeching look.

"Anything, Linda! What do you need?" He takes her hand between his two hands and smiles.

"I want a book that translates between English and German."

"You mean a dictionary? Something like that?"

"That's right. I have to understand everything that relates to my situation, and as I said, I still don't understand everything Dr. Shilling told me." She looks down at her upper body and lays a hand on her flat chest. "This I understand, I could hardly miss it." She bites her lower lip and looks earnestly at Frank. "But there was more, right? For example, what is a C-section?"

CHAPTER 48

"What, you're going alone?" Peter looks at his parents, appalled. Torr throws Claudia a look that says 'I told you so.' She puts a small suitcase on the bed and opens the closet.

"Peter, this isn't a vacation trip, we have to find out if Jasmin is still alive, and we have to talk to the police and the authorities." She is agitated as she goes through her blouses and dresses and selects a dark gray Hugo Boss sheath dress, and carefully folds it.

"It's not a vacation trip, right?" Peter glances sarcastically at the dress she has just put in the suitcase, and he gives his father a confused look. "Okay, I can get my head round that, but I'm still wondering how you are going to tell Alette. She's your daughter, not mine, luckily! At least pick me something up from GAP!" After saying that, he leaves. Claudia hears his heavy steps going downstairs, and she looks at Torr.

"He's right. What are we going to tell Alette?" She sits on the edge of the bed and puts both hands on his cheeks. "Shit, she is going to make an unforgettable scene. New York, her favorite city without her!"

Torr reaches into a drawer and pulls out a handful of briefs, then throws them casually in the open suitcase. "She'll survive it, honey, we'll let her spend the night with a friend, and stay up til ten. She will hardly be able to wait for us to go." Just as he finishes talking, the youngest Van Thiel appears in he doorway and looks from mother to father, from suitcase to suitcase.

"What's going on? Who can stay up till ten?"

Claudia's nervousness increases from minute to minute. She glances again at the saved documents on Jasmin's pen drive. It can't be a coincidence that Dr. Dubois found her address and name from Coney Island Hospital. Just, what was the connection? And where is Roberto? Why doesn't his cell number work anymore? After everything she has done for Jasmin and then for him, he just can't have gone into hiding. Mark comes into their bedroom and sits beside his mother on the edge of the bed. He has always been the sensible one of the family and really takes after his father, even if he doesn't want to hear that. "Mother, are you really sure that you aren't just chasing a false hope? I mean, none of this makes any sense!" He frowns at his mother and glances at the bright screen. She takes his hand and squeezes it.

"I have never felt so sure, Mark. She's alive, I know it! And you're right, none of this makes any sense! And that's what I want to find out in New York. I'll find her and get some answers about why she isn't contacting me, and why she is pretending something as terrible as a murder has happened! And this thing with this actor must have something to do with it." She falls back onto her pillows and runs her fingers through her blonde hair. "But how? I'll go crazy here, if we just sit around and wait!". "Mother is always right, isn't she?" He looks at her lovingly, "What's the first thing you're going to do when you get there?" Claudia looks blankly at her son, and shrugs her shoulders.

"I guess we'll go to Coney Island Hospital. Or to the Marriott Hotel. No idea, we'll talk about that on the flight. Or do you have a good suggestion?"

***

"Would you like an aperitif?" the perfectly made-up Swiss Air flight attendant gives her a friendly look.

"Absolutely, do you have a Martini?"

The dark haired woman in a suit nods and reaches for a long glass and a bottle, and asks, "With ice, or would you prefer olives?"

"Olives please." She takes the glass with colorless liquid within and the floating olives and looks at her sleeping husband beside her. "A beer for him, please." She takes a glass and puts it on the table, alongside the small screen. Business class was a good idea for her first trip without the children and she had firmly decided to make the journey following in Jasmin's footsteps. She looks again at the printed out pictures from the folder and stares at each, individual one. It wasn't just very clever of Mark, it was also the best way to start their search. Claudia doesn't notice that Torr is awake and is also looking at the pictures.

"Where did you get a picture of Roberto?" She jumps in shock as he rouses her from her thoughts with his question.

"This was one of the things on her personal pen drive. He looks like an upstanding and nice person, don't you think?" Torr takes a long swig of his beer, after they quickly clink glasses, and wipes some foam from his upper lip.

"Doesn't Frank Conley look good, too? And think how many people he kills in every film?"

"You can't seriously be comparing that! Conley is an actor! We're talking about real life here!" Claudia's shock at her husband's thoughtless words is written all over her face and she turns away, as if to protect herself from more stupidity.

"So, why do you think there are so many prisons with so many criminals inside? Don't you think that some of them have to be nice people, or at least they were at one time? You can't see into other people's souls, hon." Thinking about these words, Claudia sips at her martini and she once again wonders whose autopsy report Dr. Dubois has received.

CHAPTER 49

Frank wanted so much for Linda right then. He wanted everything, except just not that the moment would ever come that she would have to experience something so terrible. She looks at him expectantly and tries to sit up a little in bed, pain contorting her face at the attempt. "Frank, can it be worse than the fact that I don't have breasts anymore, and that I've lost my memory?" She holds his hand and tries to smile.

"Oh, Linda, it can....and I'm so sorry. The pain you are feeling comes from the C section. It's an operation where a baby is taken out of the woman's body...." He can't hold back his tears any longer and they come flowing silently from his eyes. He holds Linda's hand and strokes her head with his other hand, and holds her tight. She squeezes closed her big green eyes, and furrows her brow. Her head is turned slightly to the side and she looks at him aghast.

"I was pregnant and I had a baby?" Frank nods slowly and watches her face, so he doesn't miss her reaction. She gulps noisily and whispers, "Is it alive? Is it here? Can I see it?" Her face is a mix of hope and anxiety. Frank slowly shakes his head and leans closer to her.

"We don't know where it is. I found you, half dead on the beach, belly open and your face bashed in. Dr. Shilling detected an advanced stage of cancer in your breasts, and he had to do a mastectomy to save your life. The operation on your stomach was done halfway professionally, but not finished properly. Either it had to be done very quickly, or they didn't want you to survive...." Frank pauses and waits for Linda's reaction. He feels her hold his hand tighter, takes a deep breath and she screams, terrifyingly loudly.

***

The sedative starts working quickly and Frank lies beside Linda in bed and holds her tight, his arm around her. Her breathing is calm again, but the pain in her soul can be felt all through her body, in the form of gentle shivering and soft sobbing. What he wouldn't give to take this terrible pain away from her. A terrible fury grows within him and he picks up his Blackberry. He tries to send a message to Lou using only one hand, to ask him to bring an English/German dictionary. He had hardly sent the text before Ken's picture appears on the screen. He clicks to dismiss the call, and sends him a short text, "Linda in my arms, she knows all about baby. Can you come? Need clothes, will stay here." It didn't take more than a minute for his son to reply.

"Sure, there in approx. one hour. Shall I arrange a bigger room with an extra bed with the hospital? You need proper sleep, dad, it's not going to get any easier!"

Frank thinks for a second and types a text to say yes, then puts the cell phone on the bedside table. Linda's sobbing has stopped and Frank realizes her breathing has become deep as she has fallen deeply asleep. He slowly tries to pull his arm out from beneath her head and retreat from the embrace.

As usual, his son worked quickly and efficiently because not five minutes later Dr. Shilling appears along with two nurses. "Very good, she finds some peace when she's sleeping. Thank you very much Mr. Conley, for getting so involved, not many people would do all this! Your son has told us you would both like to be moved to a bigger room, a private room, so you can stay here. I assume you want that, too?" Frank nods exhaustedly and rubs his tired eyes.

"I have organized for her to have a German/English dictionary. It is important, from now on, that she understands everything you tell her, and I think she would like it if I can be here, whenever possible. I'd also like to be told about the stages of the chemotherapy that has been arranged, and what drugs she will be taking. It would be a good idea to have her agree to it in writing, I want her to get the best treatment, and I will pay for everything." Dr. Shilling nods understandingly and tells the nurses to get the patient ready to be moved. He tells the police officer at the door and shakes Frank's hand as he goes.

"If only everyone had as much empathy as you, Mr. Conley, the patient is very lucky to have you!"

"Linda, please call her Linda. She at least deserves a name, until we find out who she really is." Frank returns the handshake and paces beside the bed containing Linda's sleeping form.

CHAPTER 50

The Van Thiel's are standing outside the Marriott Hotel on Times Square, and they are thinking about how they should ask about Jasmin. "I'm sure they won't give out any information about their guests." Claudia gives her husband a quizzical look.

"Just let me do it, I have an idea. But you have to do what I say, without asking any questions, okay?" Torr grins at his confused wife, who nods wordlessly. They go into the hotel lobby and are immediately greeted by a concierge. They complete all the formalities and are given the keycard for their room. "Hon, you go on ahead, I'll be right with you. I just want to ask a few questions about sightseeing." Torr gives his wife the keycard for their room and nods encouragingly at her. Claudia takes her suitcase and goes off in the direction of the elevator, tossing Torr a conspiratorial smile over her shoulder as she goes. She is sure her imaginative husband will get what he is after.

Just ten minutes later, Torr comes into the hotel room where Claudia is sitting, waiting tensely on the bed and zipping through the American TV channels. She mutes the TV and turns to her husband. "So? Did you find anything out? Tell me, was she here?" Torr puts his suitcase in the corner, goes over to the bed and drops full length onto the bed.

He pulls the cover off, runs his fingers through his hair and tells her, "Yes, she was here, but only briefly. She had to be taken to the nearest hospital in the middle of the night. It seems she went into labor." Torr sits up and looks out the window. "Wow, have you seen the view? That's breathtaking! Claudia, we're in New York!" He stands up and goes to the window.

"What, how, labor, she wasn't here long? How's that possible? Tell me exactly what you asked, and what exactly the answers were! Torr, look at me, I'm going half crazy here!"

"Okay, okay. I said to the concierge that I wanted to meet my lover here a couple of weeks ago, but then something came up. I said that she made a stop here and then I didn't hear anything else from her, so I just wanted to ask if this was even the right hotel. Then what I said was, 'you know how it is, I'm here with my wife, so I'm feeling guilty,' and all that. He took pity on me and he kept looking round to make sure we weren't overheard."

224

"Honey, you're the best!" Claudia kisses him and looks at him expectantly, waiting for more details.

"So, then he told me that she had checked in and gone up to her room. Then she rang him every few minutes to ask if her husband had called. Then he said casually that he guessed she was talking about me. Her husband, but not me, so the real one, he guessed, came to reception and checked her out. He said she went to the hospital because she had gone into labor. That's it. How does that not add up, in your opinion, honey?"

Claudia paces up and down, then stops at the window. She stares pensively out at the vibrant city, "Roberto contacted us to tell us about Jasmin's death and Miriam's birth, eight days after she arrived....why did he wait more than a week after she went into labor?"

CHAPTER 51

"Dad, a dictionary?" Ken laughs happily and hands his father an iPad.

"What am I supposed to do with this?" Frank turns the iPad over in his hands and looks at it from all sides.

"It's an iPad. Don't pretend, you know exactly what it is. Lou told me you needed an English/German dictionary for Linda. Nobody uses dictionaries anymore. It takes way too long to look anything up. With this you can translate entire sentences, along with alternate translations, or look things up on the Internet in her language." Ken slaps his father heartily on the shoulder and laughs again. "Really, dad, you have to get used to new technology." Frank gives Ken the iPad back and rolls his eyes.

"You can give this thing to her yourself and explain it too. She's still sleeping, it was a big shock for her. Son, now that we know that the language she understands best is German, what can we do? What are the countries where they even speak German? Is it only Germany? I should have paid more attention in geography." Frank takes a big bite from the sandwich his son has brought for him and washes it down with a gulp of water.

"You aren't going to want to hear this, dad, but we are going to have to tell Tropman. This information will be very useful to the police. What does Dr. Shilling say about the memory loss?" The two Conleys share information about Linda's situation and what the next steps they should take are.

"Ken, nice to see you again." Linda shakes hands with the university lecturer and smiles tiredly at him. He goes to her bedside and sits down in the chair.

"Nice to see you, too. How are you?"

"I'm doing well, I've found a lot out. Do you know about the baby?" She looks at him as if the question is more rhetorical, and nods at the same time. "What's that?" she points at the iPad Ken is holding. He pushes a button on the side and holds it out to her.

"For you. This is an iPad. Here, it has an Internet connection and it will translate anything. They tell me you are gifted at languages! Say something in German for me." Ken stares expectantly at the beautiful woman in bed. She immediately starts talking to him and her face is as expressive as only the face of someone who is a master of the language can be. "Wow, that sounds amazing! What was that you said? German, just like in the book, or in the language you think in?"

Linda speaks in another language, harsh sounding and hard, and ends a sentence with, "but I don't know if it is a German dialect."

"Let's ask Google where German is spoken and how many dialects there are. I'm sure we can even find some sound files, or even videos." The knowledgeable lecturer turns the iPad so they both have a good view of it and he opens the start page of the most famous search engine on the Internet.

"Where's Frank?" Linda asks, glancing at the door.

"He's coming right back, he's phoning the police to tell them what language you speak, and that you have lost your memory. It will help them narrow down their investigation for finding out who you are."

After Frank has a surprisingly pleasant and productive conversation with Officer Tropman, he opens his contacts and rings Susie. He hears her voice after the phone rings only twice. "Who wants an interview with the hottest suspect in the whole of New York City?"

Frank grins. "That would be me! Can I tell you how impressed I am with what you did today? I heard about it from my lawyer, you put on a star performamce."

Susie's giggles, bringing him an almost forgotten feeling of joy in these dark days, and he hears her clear her throat. "It was fun, somehow. But only after the guy in the suit turned up. Wow, like in a movie, Frankie boy! Where are you, by the way?"

"I'm with Linda, have you heard that we are testing her languages?"

"Yes, your son told me what good progress you're making! You are a blessing, do you know that? I could just hug you forever, for what you're doing for the poor soul! Now, something else, my superhero. I don't know if I'm imagining this. I mean I don't really know what is happening here, and that's why I haven't told the cops anything. I mean, he still owes me a box of donuts!"

Frank laughs, "Yeah, I heard, and you're going to share them with everyone! But tell me, anything could be important, what have you found out?" He hears Susie opening a can of beer and take a swig.

"You know Bob, right?" Susie realizes that he doesn't, so she explains. "The night porter. The lonely man you met at the help desk that first evening." Frank suddenly remembers.

"Sure," he says, in anticipation of what this questionable man can contribute to answering the many questions concerning Linda.

CHAPTER 52

Claudia is sitting at the table and is bent over a spread out map of New York. "What are you looking for, honey? I thought we didn't have any time to lose here." Torr is standing with a towel round his hips, water dripping from him, in their hotel room, and he is drying his hair. "The shower is great, we should definitely get ourselves a new one." He notices that Claudia isn't listening to him and he goes over to her. A few drops fall from his hair onto the map, like rain.

"Are you crazy? What are you doing? Get lost!" His now very alert wife shoves him aside and quickly returns to the colorful and informative map in front of her. Torr shakes his head in shock, goes down on his knees beside her and asks again.

"What are you looking for?"

She is squinting at the small text, tracing a line with a pencil away from the hotel. "What do you think? The nearest hospital, obviously."

The patient husband puts his hand on hers and takes her pencil and ruler from her. "Sugar, this is all too much excitement for you, and it was a long flight, even if we were in business class. Have a hot shower, or run yourself a bath, I'm sure we have enough time for you to get a clear head, and you're going to need it."

"Yes, but first we have to find the hospital." Claudia gazes tensely at the map.

Torr follows her gaze and grins at her. "You won't find it this way. Like I said, you need a clear head!"

She looks at him, her eyes showing her irritation. "Oh, and of course your mind is clearer than mine, and you know how to find the hospital without looking at the map?"

He smiles at her triumphantly, winks at her and pulls her up out of the chair. "Off to the bathroom with you, I'll give you another chance to think about it."

***

"The nearest hospital, please," Claudia tells the cab driver, and grins at her husband, who just rolls his eyes. They sit in nervous silence in the yellow cab and try to concentrate on the streets of the exciting city.

Torr takes Claudia's hand and winks at her. "We'll find her, honey, I'm sure of it."

Claudia firmly squeezes his hand and nods absently as she gazes in the direction they are heading. She looks at the taxi driver and reads his name from the license. "Tell me, Bruno, how many hospitals are there in New York?" The driver sits up a little in his seat and glances at her in his mirror, a little surprised at her question. It seems that it is rare for him to be asked for that kind of information.

"No idea, lady, around 50, I guess," Claudia's head snaps round to face Torr, her eyes widen in shock. "I don't even know half of them. I often have to ask dispatch where exactly one of them is. We mostly work a certain district, you see? Here in Manhattan, there have to be at least ten. But it depends what kind of hospital you need. I'm driving to Lennox Hill, in the Upper Eastside, is that okay for you?"

Torr shuffles a little nearer to the driver and asks, "Why did you chose that one? Is it the nearest one to the hotel?"

"The nearest for tourists," the driver answers, with a nod, "if it isn't a real emergency. This isn't a real emergency is it?" He looks nervously in his mirror, a little confused.

Torr slumps back in his seat, looking less triumphant than just two minutes before. "No, no, we're fine, drive to Lennox Hill, thanks."

The two of them are sitting on a bench outside the entrance to the hospital. "What were we thinking? Tell me, Torr! The things you have to put up with! I'm a crazy old cow! What made me think I could find Jasmin in a city of millions! Me, a tourist? They don't even know where their own people are, here. How are they supposed to know where a pregnant Swiss lady ended up? Do you know what, let's forget it. Jasmin is dead, Miriam and Roberto are somewhere in the city, and they are building a new life without the past. I should look to the future, too. Let's forget this whole thing and enjoy our time here, seeing as we came all this way." She slaps Torr's thigh hard and is about to stand up, but her husband holds her back with a firm grip. He gives her a stern look and lifts an admonishing finger in the air.

"Wait a sec, Claudia. No way! I understand that this information isn't encouraging, but that is no reason to just give up. You can't just make me drop everything, on 48 hours notice, and drag me off to New York in the firm belief that Jasmin is here, and then give it all up because of a taxi driver! As if you could just forget all this. So stop being crazy, and listen to your gut. We are going to leave no stone unturned. So let's go into this hospital and ask about Jasmin and Dr. Shilling."

CHAPTER 53

"Look who has color in her face again, and a smile." Frank feels good as he closes the door behind him. He goes over to Linda and Ken, who are both keenly studying the iPad. Linda looks at Frank, smiles at him and waves him over.

"Hello Frank! I've missed you. Look what Ken has brought for me, I'm going to be able to get some answers with this. We're looking for more information about the treatment suggested by Dr. Shilling." She glances at the screen then turns in Frank's direction. "The doctor said you were paying for everything for me, Frank. I don't know what to say, of how I can ever thank you. I'm sure this is all going to cost a fortune, without insurance!"

Frank waves her words away and shakes his head. "Stop that. I want to do this, and I don't expect anything in return! I can afford it, and that is what I'm going to do. So what have you found out about the treatment?" A little sheepishly, and blushing as Linda takes his hand and places it against her cheek, Frank joins them in gazing at the screen.

"I've seen enough, and read enough. I'm not going to have chemotherapy." The two Conley's look at the woman in the bed as if she has just turned into a ghost. As so often, it is Ken who speaks first.

"Why have you decided not to have it?"

Linda closes her eyes, keeps Frank's big warm hand on her cheek and replies in a calm and precise tone, "I can't say for sure. Even though I don't know anymore who I am and what kind of life I have led, I feel very sure. I know I don't want chemo, and I'm going to trust that feeling. It feels like something real. Can you understand that?" She opens her eyes and looks from one surprised face to the other.

After Frank had passed on the information from the police to the two of them, each is lost in their own thoughts. "Susie just told me something strange. The night porter, Bob, is responsible for a kind of inventory. I don't understand all the details of what he's doing, but it seems a lot of things go missing from a hospital. Apart from drugs and other medical supplies, even furniture. Something struck Susie as suspicious, and she was a little perplexed. It doesn't necessarily mean anything, but something like this has never happened before...." Before Frank can continue, the door opens and Dr. Shilling comes into the room.

"Oh, how nice, everyone is here! Linda, can I call you that?" He walks to the bed with long strides and holds out his hand in greeting. She nods and shakes his hand. "Feels like your strength is returning! Wonderful! I see you're settling in well in your new room, and you're now back in contact with the outside world. Unfortunately, I don't speak German, but we have an operating room assistant here who comes from Switzerland. They speak a dialect of German there. It always makes us smile when he says a few words in his mother tongue. But let's get down to medical business, I see you are researching chemotherapy. I would be happy to talk to you about the process, if you feel up to it?" The tall doctor looks at Linda, waiting for her answer, and doesn't notice that the three of them glance at each other.

"I'm very tired and I've had enough information for one day. Is it okay if you come back tomorrow?" Linda lays her head on the pillow and gazes at the man in white.

"Of course, I understand. It's also very important that you know all the details. So it would be good if one of you two could be there?" He directs the question to the two Conleys, who both nod without hesitation. After some brief details about the coming hours, and the care and examinations she will receive from the care staff, the dedicated doctor says goodbye to the three and leaves them to their research.

"Simon Zimmermann. Here it is, I have his number! I knew I had saved it." Frank lifts his Blackberry, a smile appearing on his face. Ken is typing on the iPad at the same time, nervously holding the display where Linda can see it. She watches the short video, smiling wide and looks at Frank with tears in her eyes.

"Frank, I'm Swiss! This is my dialect!" Frank laughs, puts his Blackberry on the table and goes to her bedside! He sits next to her and takes this woman he has grown close to in his arms.

"That's great! I'm happy for you! Now we're really getting close!" His gaze turns to his son, who is standing pensive by the window, looking out into the sky. "What's wrong, Kenneth? What are you thinking about?"

His son scratches the back of his head. "Tell me again, exactly what this Simon guy wanted?" After being told the telephone call word-for-word from the start by the action hero, the lawyer shakes his head. "And you haven't told the police anything about that yet? Dad, this is very important information! And as Dr. Shilling noted, Simon worked here.

Past tense, he's gone. Something doesn't add up here. I bet this is connected somehow. I was never much good at geography, but Switzerland isn't a big country. How can this be a coincidence?" Linda and Frank look at each other in confusion. Frank suddenly stands up, but doesn't move from the spot.

"What is it, Frank?" Linda sits up in bed and lifts her arms in his direction, as if she wants to support him. He looks at her, wide eyed, and gulps before slowly speaking, "We were interrupted before. From the inventory. There is something missing... an incubator..."

CHAPTER 54

The unsuccessful couple sit exhaustedly at a small table by candlelight, in a cozy little restaurant on the Upper East Side. Claudia sips her red wine and gazes at the menu card, but her eyes are blank. Torr closes his menu and gazes at his pensive wife. "Don't feel down, honey, we just weren't prepared enough. Let me have another look at all the documents from Jasmin's computer. But first, let's order. Do you know what you want?" Claudia closes her menu and nods. They both order steak, very rare, with a big salad and another bottle of Bordeaux. While they are waiting for their food, Claudia fishes the documents out of her bag and puts them in front of Torr. He scans one page after another, then pauses at one of them. He squints and furrows his brow. He swiftly pulls one of the first pages out again, and compares the two.

"Yeesh, Claudia, how stupid can we be? It's printed right here, Coney Island Hospital! There was no need to visit any of today's hospitals. Dr. Shilling works there. That would also explain why there is no autopsy report for Jasmin, if she was never even there, but somewhere here instead. ...Shit, but is still doesn't make sense... they wouldn't just hand over a report about somebody else. Except, of course, Dr. Dubois can't speak English very well....what do you think?"

He glances at his wife, who is listening intently. "Tell me again how this doctor came to contact this Shilling? Why Coney Island? Look how far away from Manhattan it is!" He pulls the badly folded city map from his coat pocket and is about to spread it out on the table when the waiter serves their food.

After a wonderful meal, followed by a walk where they exchange ideas, the Van Thiels lie exhausted in the soft hotel bed. From habit, Torr zips through the TV channels for a while, and stops at a gossip show, his finger resting on the channel changer button. Claudia has already turned on her side, when she gets curious on hearing the name Frank Conley. "Look, honey, isn't that the action hero you were talking about." Torr's now very alert wife bolt upright in bed and stares at the screen. It's a brief report about an act of heroism by Frank Conley and, they claim, inside information that Frank has proposed to the victim on a visit to the Hamptons. The unknown beauty's memory has not returned and she has started to develop a new identity. There are various discussions about the Cinderella story, and whether Frank will become a father again at his age. They show a picture of a handsome man in a suit, who Claudia immediately recognizes from Gala as Conley's son. Torr shakes his head and switches off the television. "These Americans! I would like to know if any of that story was even true. As if it's possible, in this day and age, to not be able to identify somebody! What a crock! Good night, my beauty, tomorrow is going to be an interesting day!" He kisses his wife, who is still sitting up in bed, on the cheek, turns over, and pulls the cover up to his chin. Claudia gets up and goes to the chair she left her handbag on. She gets Jasmin's documents out and sits on the edge of the bed.

"What are you doing now? Torr switches on the bedside lamp and props himself up on his elbow so he can look at his wife.

She holds the Gala open in front of him and gazes at him in horror. "This is no accident! She taps her index finger on the photo with the caption. "Coney Island Hospital, the superhero took the victim there!"

Torr stares at his wife in surprise. "You aren't saying that Jasmin could be the victim? Claudia, please, you don't really believe this story, do you? Honey, you know how many stories we make up in advertising to get the ratings we need? This is just marketing, I promise you! Look, this Conley is an old actor who has gone out of fashion. That's why a new story has been put out there, to keep his name in circulation, and keep film offers coming in. Honestly, how can you fall for this? Now get some sleep, we'll go to Coney Island Hospital tomorrow and ask for Dr. Shilling. And you can ask him about Franky Boy, too!" Torr laughs, pats his wife's hand and lies back in the soft pillows.

Claudia picks the magazine back up and looks at the picture again. She puts it on the bedside table and snuggles under the covers. Torr could be right, that magazines are so successful only because there are lots of gullible people, like her. But what if he's wrong and Conley's Jane Doe is Jasmin. She wonders if she will be able to get to her if that is the case. Via the Swiss embassy? The consulate? Or will they just laugh at her, like her husband, the advertising expert, just did? She is the first to admit she's a fool! If the Americans are so addicted to the media, they would have reported about Miriam. Or was that what they meant when they asked if Frank was going to be a father again?

CHAPTER 55

Frank and Ken take advantage of the time when Linda is being examined and freshened up to visit their important friend, Susie. The action hero contacts the police and tells them in detail about the last few hours of recent past. "Hey dad, aren't there any offers of new films on the horizon? Or have you retired without me realizing because you have had enough of the celebrity lifestyle?" Kenneth winks at his father and takes him by the shoulder.

"There have been some offers! I'm not that old yet!" He lovingly punches his son on the arm as they leave the elevator and enter the reception area. "But none of them has grabbed me, my head is somewhere else right now." He squints, looking for Susie off in the distance. "I will admit my body is showing signs of age. I need glasses, for example. Is she there?" Ken throws his head back and laughs.

"You'll hear for yourself soon enough!" he says. "Her majesty is approaching!"

"And I thought I had been tossed aside, now that the little mouse has a voice! So, you two spying on us all? Or are you just visiting old Susie in the hopes of some donuts?" The visibly excited reception lady reaches for a box behind her, then opens it on the counter in front of the Conleys, "That nosy cop kept his promise and he brought me these tasty treats. Help yourselves! We deserve it! So what's going on with you two? Have you found out anything else?" Susie grabs herself a sticky, pink doughnut and takes a big bite, while she looks expectantly from one to the other.

Frank and Kenneth both also help themselves to a tasty doughnut, even though Frank is already regretting it as soon as he has bitten into it. He starts having trouble swallowing it down. He puts it on a napkin alongside the box and starts to tell Susie the latest information, "Yes, we've made a lot of progress. Linda comes from Switzerland. We found out because of her accent."

"Oh, from Switzerland! I bet they have real nice chocolate there! Expensive though! But keep talking, you health freak!" She glances disapprovingly at the doughnut with a bite taken out of it that is lying on the desk between them.

"I'm sorry, Susie, I just can't eat stuff like that, no matter how hard I try." Frank gently shakes his head, hoping she will take pity on him.

"Don't worry," she tells him, "all the more for me! You stay sexy! Okay, so Switzerland! But still no memory? Nothing?"

The action hero grins thankfully at the ruler of reception and shakes his head. "Nothing. Nothing at all. My son brought her a little computer."

"An iPad, dad!" Ken grins between bites of doughnut.

"Yes, one of those, and now she can look anything up on the Internet, and check up on her treatment. And now she knows about her pregnancy and the missing baby. It's horrible Susie, what this poor young woman has been through!"

Susie closes her eyes and puts her hand on her heart. "Poor little thing! How nice that she has two knights in shining armor! What you two are doing is wonderful! I'm so proud of you! What did the police say?"

"Now they can really narrow their search. They can check the airports and borders for people who came in from Switzerland. But, you know, they used acid on her fingerprints, so it was somebody who knew what they were doing. Her eyes could be the key. They forgot about that, these assholes. Excuse my language! But this will all take a while, you now the authorities. It's the first time I'm glad that Tropman is the aggressive type! That will be a big help to us, I'm telling you!" The two people listening nod, lost in thought, then Frank's cell rings. He pulls it out of his breast pocket and answers.

"Hello?" Frank listens to the caller, nodding tensely, closes his eyes and bites his lower lip. "Okay, I understand. Of course I can. I'll ask her as soon as I see her again. No, not right now. Okay, thank you, officer, you'll hear from me." He presses the button on his Blackberry to end the call and puts it on the reception desk. "Speak of the devil. Nobody in Switzerland is listed as missing who matches Linda's description. But they have sent her picture to the Swiss police. They are going to keep looking. No nameless babies have been reported here in New York, nor any suspicious registrations of birth."

Ken abruptly interrupts his father, "Wait a minute, of course newborn babies are registered in their parents' name. There must be a birth certificate. Have they checked all the hospitals that have issued birth certificates in the past two months? There has to have been some trick here, unless...."

Susie suddenly grabs Ken's hand, "A blood test could have identified the father of the baby!" She looks at Frank with wide eyes and continues, "What else did he say, sugar?"

"He asked me if, for security reasons, I could take Linda home with me. Dr. Shilling says she's stable and she can be moved, and she could be regularly examined there. Tropman thinks she's in danger as long as she's here. The media are too interested, and that's my fault, unfortunately. But he says this attention could be made to work in our favor. She'll be safer at home with me."

CHAPTER 56

The yellow cab stops right outside the main entrance of Coney Island Hospital and the driver gratefully accepts the fare and the generous tip from Torr. Claudia is already waiting at the door, which opens as if by magic, and she gazes within. Her husband gives her a gentle nudge as he passes and nods toward reception. She closes her eyes for a fraction of a second, takes a deep breath, and follows him determinedly in the direction of the latest lead they are hanging their hopes on. The man behind reception puts the phone down, shakes his head and turns to the visitors. "How can I help you?"

"We'd like to see Dr. Shilling," Torr says confidently, and he glances at Claudia.

The man, who is wearing a security guard's uniform looks very tired, "Do you have an appointment? Nobody told me about a meeting with the doctor," he says, subdued and frowning, as he searches for a pencil and pad behind reception. "what was your name?"

Torr interrupts his search. "We don't have an appointment, it's sort of an emergency."

The hospital employee tuts in annoyance and glances from Claudia to Torr, his eyes wide. "So what kind of emergency is it, may I ask?"

Claudia can no longer hold back her tears. She goes to the chairs in the waiting area, sits and sobs desperately, her face in her hands. Torr now looks at the surprised man behind reception with a look of shock on his face, and he starts to tell their story. The appalled listener keeps glancing at Claudia and shakes his head sympathetically.

"I'm very sorry, that all sounds terrible. But you're talking to the wrong guy here. I'm just here to cover the night shift, you're here too early." He glances at his inexpensive watch, purses his lips and continues, "The reception lady will be here in about an hour, and she'll be able to help you because it's her job to operate this damn thing, here." He pats the top of the computer with a big, fleshy hand. "Don't get me wrong, I'd love to help you two, but there are rules I have to follow. I can only let people in if they have an appointment."

Torr's head sinks for a moment, then he looks deep in the eyes of the man on the other side of the counter. "I understand, rules are rules. In an hour you say? And you think this woman will let us talk to Dr. Shilling without an appointment?" He glances at the man's name badge and adds, "Bob?"

At the sound of his name, Bob clears his throat, pulls his wrinkled pants up a bit and looks round cautiously to make sure nobody can overhear. "Well, you see, Susie, that is Susan Manders, is really unbelievable. She even came here one day from the police station in a luxury limo, and the police officer personally sent her a box of doughnuts. She can wrap anyone round her little finger!" Bob briefly laughs out loud and leans toward Torr. "She was in pretty much all the newspapers, but she's so humble! She's become a real celebrity! But she's still so down to earth, and she doesn't have it easy with her two boys. A working mother, all alone...." The telephone interrupts the torrent of his words, as he picks up the receiver, he holds his finger in the air self-importantly, ordering Torr to wait.

Torr just nods and quickly goes over to his wife, who is still crying, takes her by the arm, and hurries her out the door. Claudia's face doesn't look sad, or exhausted, or angry, it is more a confused shock as she gazes at her husband. Torr's face is dark red, his neck red and blotchy, tears of mirth rolling down his cheeks, a raw chuckling audible from his throat. He has his hand on his stomach, and Claudia grasps him by the shoulder and yells at him.

"What the...have you gone crazy?? What's going on?? Have you lost your mind?? Stop it, you're scaring me!" At her words, Torr tries to pull himself together, with difficulty.

"I'm sorry, honey, wait, I'm getting it together!" He holds his wife by the arm with one hand and uses the other to wipe the tears from his face. "I'm okay. I'm okay! All right." As he is talking, he can't help another short burst of laughter, but again manages to pull himself together. He throws his head back and looks at the sky. "Oh my god, Claudia! There are people who are so stupid you just wouldn't believe it! The next time somebody starts talking about stupid Americans, I'm going to find it more difficult to criticize them! They really exist! I have to use this for an advertisement, it's so funny!" Before another fit of laughter and tears can overtake him, the advertising executive takes a deep breath, gives his wife a pleased look and says, "You aren't crazy, you wonderful woman! That guy in there is, and he gets paid for it! Your inquisitive, bloodhound nose is leading you in the right direction! Dr. Shilling works here, and so does the enigmatic lover of that actor from the gossip pages! She's the receptionist here, and she'll arrive in an hour." He grabs Claudia by the shoulders, to try and shake the quizzical look from he face. "Don't you understand? The enigmatic victim is, or was, here and Susie, as he calls her, knows everything and she can work wonders!" He shakes his head, as if trying to concentrate only on what is essential, then adds, "I believe we have found Jasmin. At the very least I think we will very soon be talking to somebody who knows where she is!"

CHAPTER 57

Frank is about to open the door to Linda's private room but Leslie comes out of the room just at that moment. "Frank! Kenneth, it's lucky I met you! I was just Dadping in to see Linda." She reaches out to shake hands with both Conleys, then hurries away on her cloud-silent shoes. "Best wishes to you both! See you later!" She quickly disappears, too quickly, Frank thinks, as he watches her get into the elevator and go off to her ward. Frank looks back toward the room and it takes only a fraction of a second for him to take in what he is looking at. Linda is sitting in a wheelchair at the window, the iPad in her lap and her wide eyes staring at him.

"Linda, you're out of bed! Hey, so what's going on here?" He quickly goes over to the wheelchair, from where two beautiful dark green eyes are regarding him.

"Why didn't you tell me?" she asks, in her cute English accent.

"What are you talking about, Linda?" Frank squats down beside the wheelchair and holds on tight to it.

"All this, here!" Linda picks up the iPad and turns it so he can see the screen. The action hero sees several pictures of himself, taken from the media, with Susie and with his son outside court, along with a few images from his movies and from gala evenings.

"What exactly do you mean, Linda?" She briefly throws her head back and laughs, then looks at him with her eyebrows raised.

"I mean the fact that you are world famous, for example! And this stuff here, about how you have had a lot of trouble because of me, and not just you, also an innocent woman!? Isn't that enough?"

She looks from Frank to Kenneth, who is calmly watching the situation unfold from a distance. Frank stands up, shoots Ken a reproachful look and says, "The Internet......what a wonderful invention!" He reaches for a chair and sits directly opposite Linda. After he has explained all the gossip in the media, and Susie's innocence, Frank takes Linda's hand in his and leans over to her, "Listen, Linda, Officer Tropman asked me if I would take you home with me, until we know more about you and what happened to you. What do you say? Do you trust me enough to come home with me?" He looks her in the eye, but he sees that she is tearing up. "Is everything okay, Linda? What is going on?" He shuffles nearer to her wheelchair in his chair and gently strokes her cheek.

"Everything's okay. It's just that I don't know how I will ever be able to thank you for what you are doing for me here! I mean, you don't even know me. I'm not just a stranger to myself, but to everyone. And, despite all that, you want to take me home with you, even though you're world famous! And who am I? Somebody without a name, without a past, with a criminal past....!"

Linda's sobbing almost brings Frank and Ken to tears, too. But they both pull themselves together and Frank determinedly attempts to get the situation back under control with a joke. "This is what I'm hearing, 'you want to take me home with you.' That's what you said. That, to my ears, is very clearly a yes! Ken, lets go home! With Linda! Can you check us out please? We want to get out of this hospital, right?" He winks to Linda, who is wiping tears from her cheeks and nods joyfully.

"Yes, let's get out of here!"

Ken holds the room door open for Frank, who is pushing Linda out into the corridor in the wheelchair. "Everything sorted out with Dr. Shilling?" Frank just shoots Ken a brief look. "Just so nobody says we abducted you!

That would fit with this soap opera, right?" He gently shoves Linda from behind and grins.

"It's all good! He sends his apologies for not being able to be here, but he says he will call in on Linda for an examination in two weeks. Until then, all the best and we will be in touch with him as soon as any memories return!" They go together to the elevator and wait for the doors to open, while Linda looks round and gazes at Frank.

"Do you think it might be possible to meet this Susie person?"

"Of course you can!" the action hero says, grinning, "It won't even take five minutes, and I'll introduce you! She'll be looking forward to meeting you!" He pushes the wheelchair into the open elevator, where all three run into Leslie again.

"So, where are you going? You're going home? They didn't say you were being released today." Leslie excitedly looks from Linda to Frank and to Ken. Linda frowns and looks at Frank in surprise, then raises her eyebrows as she answers Leslie.

"I didn't know myself until just now! Yes, I'm going home!" Frank gently squeezes her shoulder as she says these words and looks at the floor indicator in the elevator.

"Oh wow! Your memory is back! Congratulations! Where is it you're going then?" Leslie's exaggerated tone seems to reverberate from the walls of the elevator, and she seems to become aware of it from the confused looks on the faces of the three people she is talking to. She clears her throat and quickly looks down, with the words, "Sorry, that's none of my business!" The elevator stops on the second floor and Leslie again pushes past the two Conleys and hurries out, murmuring "Best of luck," as she disappears down a corridor that is not part of her department.

CHAPTER 58

To avoid having to run into the extremely talkative Bob at reception, after leaving him so rudely, Claudia and Torr decide to go for a walk in the area round the hospital. As they walk, the advertising executive tells his wife in detail what he has learned from the security guard, "You see, honey, this has to be connected to Jasmin! Your feeling was right, this can't be a coincidence." Torr takes hold of his exhausted wife by the arm and pulls her close, then hugs her. "Jasmin is alive, and you'll see her again soon, I promise!"

Claudia enjoys the energy the hug gives her and sobs silently to herself. "I want that so bad! But Torr, what can be going on with Roberto? He can't have just disappeared with Miriam? Don't they have things organized here, I mean, how is this possible?" She looks at her husband with teary eyes.

He lovingly wipes the tears from her cheeks and kisses her gently on the mouth. "We'll find that out, too, all in good time. But for now, lets just concentrate on Jasmin and work out how we are going to get to this enigmatic Susie. You know what she looks like, right?"

Claudia nods and murmurs to herself, "Definitely not like Conley's lover..."

Torr takes a quick look through the front door, then goes back to Claudia on the bench in front of the entrance. "The coast is clear, there's a woman at reception, maybe in her 50s. Librarian glasses and a little chubby. Could that be her?"

Claudia nods eagerly and nervously. "So should we just be straight with her?"

Torr nods emphatically. "Yes, yes, absolutely! She must be quite a lady, judging by the way Bob was saying. So we'll just spill our guts and see what she says! We'll make it! This is why we're here, don't forget that!" He lovingly takes his wife's hand, squeezes it determinedly and walks triumphantly with her through the big glass doors of Coney Island Hospital.

"Hello, and welcome to Coney Island Hospital, how can I help you?" the woman at reception says, smiling at the two tourists from behind her glasses and the reception desk. Claudia takes a deep breath, lays her hands flat on the counter and briefly closes her eyes. The friendly reception lady suddenly stands up, puts a hand on top of Claudia's, reaches for the phone with the other and says, "Do you feel okay, sugar? Do you need a doctor?"

Claudia opens her eyes, and waves her hand away from the phone. "No, no, I'm okay, everything's fine with me. Susie? Are you Susie?" She looks at the reception lady sadly, but full of hope.

Susie slowly takes her glasses from her nose and lets them drop, to dangle on their chain, before nodding and smiling. "Well, you seem to know who I am, so who are you, sugar? And, of course, who is your handsome friend?" She glances at Torr, then returns her full attention to Claudia.

Claudia puts a hand on Susie's, which is still on top of her own. "I'm Claudia Van Thiel," she says, "and this is my husband, Torr. Susie, we desperately need your help to find our, I mean my, friend. We came from Switzerland especially, and now we're here with you, our last hope of ever seeing her again!"

Susie frowns, and looks from Claudia to Torr and back. "From Switzerland, you say? What makes you think I know where your friend is? What's her name?"

"Jasmin, she's called Jasmin Steiner. I have information about a man called Dr. Shilling. And, well we have gossip magazines in Switzerland, too. Your picture was in it, in a story about a strange victim and the same hospital as this Dr, Shilling and..." Claudia has to pause for breath,

Susie gently pats her hand and talks to her in a soothing tone of voice.

"Take it easy, sugar, take it easy. If Susie can help, then you can be sure she will. Let me get this straight. You're looking for your friend, Jasmin, and you think she's here because you saw me in a gossip magazine? I don't understand what you're talking about, and I've got a very quick mind!" She grins at Claudia. "So when was the last time you saw your friend, and where was it?"

She gets a piece of paper and a pen, and starts to take note of what Claudia is telling her. With Claudia's last sentence she puts the pen down, the blood draining from her face, and takes her glasses off. "You Swiss people are real good at making chocolate, right? The kind of friend I've been searching for since kindergarten! Sugar, I think you've hit pay dirt! Let me make a call." With these words she leaves the hopeful looking Van Thiels at reception and disappears into a back room.

CHAPTER 59

Linda is standing on a wide terrace with an unrestricted view of a calm sea. Her gaze is empty and sad, as Frank moves to stand beside her and puts a protective arm round her shoulder. "How is the pain? Are you okay without the wheelchair?"

She smiles at him tiredly and lays her head on his chest. "It's bearable. My heart is a lot more painful. Frank, will I ever be able to hold my child in my arms?" She closes her eyes, breathes the fresh sea air and Frank's comforting scent.

He holds her closer and strokes her dark, soft hair with his free hand. "I'll do everything I can to make that happen! You have to rest, enjoy the fresh air and remember to do your brain training. I'll put some music on, anything that might help your memory to come back. Tropman is coming round again this afternoon, so we'll find out the latest from the police. After that, I'll make a couple of calls and we'll really get the ball rolling! You can count on me! They won't get away so easily!"

Linda gives him a hopeful smile and winks at him. "You actors don't have much to do, do you?"

He smiles charmingly and raises an eyebrow before replying, "You just have to know how!" The action hero hugs Linda tighter and closes his eyes, so he can enjoy the moment, breathing the fresh air and experiencing the closeness of her body.

***

Just as Linda is making herself comfortable in a chair on the beach, Frank calls to her from the house and waves to her to come. "Tropman is here," she mutters and gets up, pain clearly visible on her face. She walks slowly toward the house, with Freja alongside, like a close friend. She enters the large living room through the open patio door, and sees Frank, Officer Tropman, another police officer and two men wearing suits. Linda walks confidently toward the officer she already knows and reaches out to shake his hand. "It's nice to see you again, officer!"

The police officer smiles at Linda in admiration and returns her greeting. "The pleasure is all mine. You look great! The sea air is really doing you good, right!?"

She nods, and looks at the two men in suits. "And who are you?"

But her question doesn't get answered, and she ends up just waiting for somebody to react. It is Tropman who breaks the silence. "Let me introduce special agents Mayer and Cooper. They are from a special unit and they will be taking over your case from now on. The Coney Island Police transferred your case to them, because an out of state and an international search will be necessary, which is unfortunately beyond our capabilities. Do you understand what I'm saying?" He looks at Linda for an answer, who replies with only a tired smile, her gaze still fixed on the two silent men.

"If I understand correctly, that means you still don't know anything at all. You don't have my baby, or the..." Her voice quavers and she looks to Frank for help.

He immediately goes over to her. "Do you have any leads at all?" he asks, as he takes her in his arms.

Linda lies on the chaise longue by the fireplace, exhausted, pulls the blanket up to her chin and closes her stinging eyes. Her tears flow over her cold cheeks and she tries to take deep breaths. She hears Frank moving around in the kitchen, and she is glad that she has the ordeal of unanswered questions with no new information behind her again. Her endless disappointment slowly starts to turn into rage, and she wonders what she can do to get her revenge. Frank appears beside her, holding two glasses of water with mint leaves and lemon slices.

"Here, you need to drink something, it'll do you good. It will work out, Linda. You're safe here and you can rest and recuperate. You're not alone, remember that." He gently strokes her hair and kisses her softly on the forehead. He goes over to the entertainment center. Pushes a couple of buttons and turns the volume knob. Soft piano music can be heard across the room, becoming a floating cloud of weightless contentment. Frank sits in one of the tasteful chairs, takes a long sip of his water, closes his eyes and listens to the music. It is the first bars of "Fuer Elise", which Frank considers a masterpiece. He is lost in the music when he hears Linda suddenly gasp for air. He jumps to his feet, runs over to her and holds her tight, "Linda? Linda? Are you okay? What's the matter?"

CHAPTER 60

Claudia and Torr are sitting on uncomfortable chairs in the waiting area of the police station on Coney Island. They are even more agitated now, after their encounter with Susie, and for the first time Claudia is starting to think they might be nearing their objective. Susie's positive and extremely open attitude has given her so much hope. Susie didn't say anything concrete to them, but Claudia feels she is not far away from looking Jasmin in her lively and beautiful eyes again. She takes Torr's hand, which is beating out a nervous tune on his lap, and lovingly squeezes it. He gives her an excited look and kisses her on the cheek.

"Mr and Mrs. Van Thiel?" says a uniformed police officer with small, beady eyes, standing in front of them with legs akimbo, and hands on his hips. They both immediately jump to their feet, so they can speak to him, eye to eye. "Do you speak English?" Torr says they do. "Okay, follow me," he gestures to a woman at a desk and, as he walks by, he says, "We don't need a translator, but some water would be great. Or would you prefer a coffee? Though I would advise against it, this isn't a coffee shop and the muck you get from the machine here tastes awful." He is talking over his shoulder to them, and they decline his offer.

The policeman opens a door into a long corridor, goes to a room and motions for them to take a seat. The cold room reminds Claudia of all the movies she has seen where the police interview criminals, victims and witnesses. An uneasy feeling starts to grow within her, and she wonders if any innocent people have ever been charged with crimes here, just because they were scared of saying the wrong thing.

Officer Tropman looks at his notes, taps his pencil nervously on the table and scratches his neck. "Okay, let me get this straight. You both live in Switzerland and your heavily pregnant boss came to New York about four months ago." For the umpteenth time, he picks up printouts of the documents Claudia has from Jasmin's computer. "You found these documents on your superior's computer, and they include the name of a Dr. Shilling, who works here at Coney Island Hospital, and who was recommended to Mrs. Steiner by her gynecologist. You know there's a connection because you were told she was suffering from aggressive breast cancer, and she was advised against taking the trip. But she wanted to travel anyway, and see her husband and his friend, who also works at Coney Island Hospital, though you don't know his name. You have had contact with Mrs. Steiner's husband, who has a different surname. He's called

Garreffa, and his first name is Roberto. He told the school director about the death of his wife, and he also told him that their child, Miriam, had survived, despite being premature. So you cleared the couple's apartment and held a memorial celebration so friends and relatives in Switzerland could say their goodbyes. The husband decided to take a job at a hospital here in New York, and start a new life with his daughter, and now you can't get hold of him. The gynecologist received an autopsy report that he had doubts about, because some of the operations she had already and that he knew about were not mentioned......"

Claudia is paying attention to every word, to be sure that Officer Tropman has understood everything. But now the strange feeling in her stomach is getting stronger, and she starts to feel like she shares some blame for what happened. 'You cleared the couple's apartment,' from his mouth the words sound like an accusation. You 'held a memorial celebration,' now she starts to really feel ill. She had buried Jasmin alive and mourned for her. Claudia suddenly stands up, holds both hands to her mouth and manages to squeak the word, "Toilet," through her fingers.

Claudia looks in the mirror and sees her face is white as a sheet. She hadn't realized until this moment how naive and extremely stupid her heartfelt and well-intentioned support of Roberto actually was. How could he have fooled her without a second thought, and got her to help him escape and go underground? She hits the hand dryer with her balled fist and it makes a dull, humming noise.

The door opens and the female police officer who escorted her to the toilet glances inside. "Everything okay in here?"

Claudia nods, sighs, and goes out past the young woman into the corridor. The door to the interview room is opened for her and she finds Torr sitting inside alone. He immediately stands up, goes to her and puts a hand on his wife's shoulder.

"Everything okay, honey? You ready to go again? Did you puke all over the police bathroom?" He throws his head back and laughs, briefly but heartily. "Oh, my love, you're priceless! Come and sit down. Officer Tropman went through our documents a little more, then he said he had to go and make a phone call. In the meantime, if you're up to it, he wants you to think about whether Jasmin has any distinguishing features. Unique characteristics, you know what I mean? Like a visible scar or a birth mark, that sort of thing. They could be helpful in identifying her."

Claudia's eyes go wide and she grips Torr's arm tightly. "What, do they have somebody who might fit? I mean, did he give anything away, where... who? I knew the nice receptionist from Coney Island Hospital wouldn't have sent us to the police otherwise. She knows more than she is saying, and so does Tropman! Torr, they know! They know they have my Jasmin!"

CHAPTER 61

Dr. Shilling gently closes the door after examining Linda and meets Frank on the sweeping marble staircase.

They go down to the living room together, where the doctor puts his bag on the floor and looks through the big window at the Atlantic, a look of concentration on his face. "Dr. Shilling?" Frank murmurs gently. "What was that? Does she have to go back to hospital? Or should you be examining her every day?"

The doctor shakes his head, almost imperceptibly, and answers Frank in a calm, professional tone. "No, no, there's absolutely no need for her to return to the hospital. Since she moved here with you she has been making very good progress. I can't explain what kind of episode that was. She is fine now. She said the police were here again, still no new information?" He gazes at Frank expectantly.

Frank rests his hands on his hips and nods. "That's right, no new information, unfortunately. My son and I have to think about what else we can do, even maybe including the media. This is all taking too long and who knows what they are doing with the baby. This is no way for Linda to live!" He opens the top button of his shirt, as if he needs more air, then adds, "Dr. Shilling, what do you think... Will her memories ever come back?" His expression shows how hopeless and helpless he feels.

The doctor again shakes his head, hardly perceptibly, and shrugs his shoulders. "God alone knows. From a medical point of view, there is nothing wrong with her, and the neurologists agree. There is no injury to the brain, no bleeding on the brain, which is very lucky, when you remember how badly beaten she was. So the cause of the amnesia must be the shock and the trauma. When the time is right, she will have to start visiting a psychiatrist, and a trauma specialist. First she will have to feel fit enough, physically. I'll email you the details of some good people later today. Mr. Conley, I have to get going, it's not really my job to be doing house calls out in the Hamptons." The tall, friendly doctor grins and heads for the patio door, as he goes he says, "Although I have to admit it is exciting to be whisked from the hospital by helicopter!"

Frank's Blackberry starts vibrating and he pulls it out, "Officer Tropman, I hope you're calling with good news!" Frank sits, a little out of breath, in a leather chair and closes his eyes to give the caller his full attention. Not twenty seconds later, his lids open and he stands up straight as an arrow. His heart suddenly starts hammering, even though he hasn't been doing any exercise, seemingly loud enough to be heard throughout the room. As if the caller could see him, he nods emphatically and holds his free hand in front of his mouth and concentrates on sucking on his lower lip.

"Yes, I'm still here. This is amazing! Of course we can come to the police station. Do we have permission to land? Okay, wonderful. We'll be with you in an hour. What can I say to Linda? Okay, I understand, I think that's best. See you soon, Officer!" Frank ends the call with shaky fingers and looks up at the floor above, where Linda has gone to rest. Slowly at first, then with ever faster steps, he goes up the marble stairs and knocks on the door of the suite of rooms that are now Linda's living area.

"Linda, sweetheart, are you asleep?" he says through the door. There isn't a sound to be heard, or any answer. He knocks again, a little louder, and he calls her name. Again there is no answer. Frank slowly turns the gold handle and opens the door a little, just enough for him to poke his head through the gap and take a look. Linda is nowhere to be seen, neither in bed, nor at the desk, or even on the small balcony. His searching gaze goes in the direction of the bathroom, where the door is wide open but no sound is coming out. "Linda? Are you here? Hello?" Frank opens the door the whole way and goes across the room into the bathroom and the changing room. No sign of her. "Dammit, Linda!" Frank's shock makes his voice sharp and he quickly goes out to the stairs. "Linda! Where are you?" he runs down to the sauna, the home cinema, the pool, then back up to the living room, through the kitchen and out onto the patio. Linda is nowhere to be found. He feels another dose of adrenaline hit his blood and spread through his system. He gets his Blackberry out of his pant pocket then hastily dials a stored number, which immediately connects him with the sound of his son's voice.

"Dad, I'm sure! It makes a lot of sense, come on, we'll meet there. I'm leaving now. Make sure to bring Freja and remember to breathe, dad! Everything is going to be okay! Everything is definitely going to be okay!" At Kenneth's comforting words and the sound of his voice, Frank's body and his mind start to relax a little, and a lot of the fear that is threatening to overwhelm him dissipates, at least for a while. He calls his pilot and asks him to get the helicopter ready to fly.

"Freja, old girl, come on, we're going out to bring Linda home. We won't be in the air long, my big girl, don't be frightened, you'll be fine. But we have to hurry." He pulls on a thin windbreaker, slips on a pair of trainers, and puts on his New York Rangers cap, then gets the leash from its hook. They both go out onto the patio, then through the drizzle to the helicopter pad, where they wait for their ride, which can already be heard approaching.

"Frank, get in! I'm going to be earning my money tonight! What has Lou got to say about it?" Mike smiles and waves at the two men in the thundering helicopter. Frank gets Freja into the chopper behind him while he sits beside the grinning pilots, closes the door, buckles up, puts on his headphones, and adjusts the mic, "We're flying to Coney Island Beach. I hope you find a good place to land, near the pier at the amusement park. In this weather, there will be hardly anyone on the beach," Frank says into his microphone, and watches his house shrink and disappear below them.

***

Frank can hear Ken's steps in the distance, and he hurries over to him, along with Freja. The two Conleys embrace and Ken slaps his father on the shoulder, still trying to keep him calm. "Dad, it's time. We're almost at the finishing line." He nods in the direction of the huge Coney Island pier. Frank's eyes follow his gaze and he sees a woman standing there.

He squints a little and says, mostly to himself rather than to Ken, "Is that Linda? But how did she know....?"

Ken still has his hand on his father's shoulder, and he gives it a squeeze as he gazes at the boardwalk, too. "Because she remembers, dad. That woman there isn't Linda anymore, that's Jasmin Steiner. Take Freja with you, she'll help break the ice. Get going, already!" The clever lawyer gives his father a shove and waves him lovingly on his way.

***

The empty and unreal mournfulness within me can't be described. I can't even say if it is sadness. It is a combination of rage, indignation, pain, sadness, aggression, frustration, endless incomprehension, disappointment and desperation. A feeling of hatred wells up within me the like of which I have never before felt in my life. My life has been stolen from me because of an equal amount of disappointment, hate, rage and endless incomprehension. Now I am standing here on this pier, where my body was dumped. They wanted to give me to the waves here, thrown to be eaten by the Atlantic. Bound like an animal while they played god and ripped a second life, a pure soul, from my body.

I will never let you get away with this. I will get my child back and throw you to the wolves. With Frank at my side, I can regain my courage and my power, and put an end to this horror. I feel for the big, warm hand on my shoulder, gently kiss it and turn to face my savior. With tears in my eyes, we gaze at each other a long time in silence, until he takes me in his arms, close to his powerfully thumping heart.

"Hello Jasmin. It is a pleasure to meet you! I'm Frank." He lovingly strokes my hair and squeezes me tight again.

"I'm Linda, Jasmin doesn't exists anymore, Frank. Let's go see Tropman, there is somebody we urgently have to catch up with."

Frank loosens his embrace and looks at me questioningly. "Who are you talking about?"

I stroke Freja's head, look in the direction of the mainland and answer. "Susie will have to say goodbye to her friend......Leslie knows where Roberto and my child are!"

Outroduction

She looks so much like her father. Roberto would have made a very beautiful woman. That stupid, lovesick Italian. It didn't have to end this way, you sensitive dog! Our plan would have worked perfectly, Leslie and I were perfectly prepared. But no, he had to get involved, suddenly full of regret and sympathy. Shame about him, an absolute shame about him. He was always a good friend to me and he would also have become a good colleague at Coney Island Hospital.

"Yes, little one, are you hungry? Daddy has warmed a bottle. Here.....yes, that's right. My big girl, getting better every day. And mom will be with us soon, then we'll look for a beautiful house with a big garden for you. Daddy will definitely be able to find a new job then. I'm sure they need operating room assistants here in Mexico......."

About the author:

Hiam Mondini was born in Switzerland.

Writting and music were her favourite courses while studying to be a teacher. Hiam's diverse career path included working as a teacher, a Human Resources Assistant, head of Diversity&Health Management in a Swiss bank, Managing Director and Make-up Artist.

After being faced with personal tragic events, Hiam had the same reoccurring dream over and over again. She finally decided to write it down and share it in her first novel with the world.

Herstellung und Verlag:
BoD - Books on Demand, Norderstedt
ISBN 978-3-7460-8126-7